FINALE

FINALE

THE LOST DECADES OF UNCLE CHOW TUNG

IAN HAMILTON

SPIDERLINE

Published in Canada in 2022 and the USA in 2022
by House of Anansi Press Inc.
www.houseofanansi.com

House of Anansi Press is committed to protecting our natural environment.
This book is made of material from well-managed FSC®-certified forests,
recycled materials, and other controlled sources.

House of Anansi Press is a Global Certified Accessible™ (GCA by Benetech)
publisher. The ebook version of this book meets stringent accessibility
standards and is available to students and readers with print disabilities.

26 25 24 23 22   1 2 3 4 5

Library and Archives Canada Cataloguing in Publication
Title: Finale : the lost decades of Uncle Chow Tung / Ian Hamilton.
Names: Hamilton, Ian, 1946- author.
Identifiers: Canadiana (print) 2022015726X | Canadiana (ebook)
20220157294 | ISBN 9781487010188 (softcover) |
ISBN 9781487010195 (EPUB)
Classification: LCC PS8615.A4423 F56 2022 | DDC C813/.6—dc23

Book design: Alysia Shewchuk

*House of Anansi Press respectfully acknowledges that the land on which
we operate is the Traditional Territory of many Nations, including the
Anishinabeg, the Wendat, and the Haudenosaunee. It is also the Treaty
Lands of the Mississaugas of the Credit.*

 Canada Council
for the Arts Conseil des Arts
du Canada   ONTARIO ARTS COUNCIL
CONSEIL DES ARTS DE L'ONTARIO
an Ontario government agency
un organisme du gouvernement de l'Ontario

With the participation of the Government of Canada
Avec la participation du gouvernement du Canada | Canadä

*We acknowledge for their financial support of our publishing program the Canada
Council for the Arts, the Ontario Arts Council, and the Government of Canada.*

Printed and bound in Canada

For my three clever, loving, and supportive daughters:
Jill Hamilton, Stephanie Woodward, and Alexis Pinson.

CHOW TUNG, A MAN MOST PEOPLE CALLED UNCLE, WAS walking along a street in the town of Fanling, in Hong Kong's New Territories. He wasn't sure why he was there, other than that he had an irresistible urge for a plate of Dong's chicken feet.

Uncle had lived in Fanling for forty-five years before moving to Kowloon eleven years ago. He had left of his own choosing, and none of his friends and colleagues in the Fanling Heaven and Earth Society, also known as the triads, would have objected in the least if he had stayed. Uncle had been the leader, the Mountain Master, of the Fanling Triad for more than thirty years, and had made it the wealthiest and most respected gang in all of Hong Kong. Because of his foresight, the Fanling Triad was guaranteed a secure future.

He had first started to delegate some of his Mountain Master responsibilities when he was elected chairman of the triad societies, a position he had helped create to resolve disputes among the more than twenty gangs that existed in Hong Kong. When Uncle's second two-year term as chairman had expired, it was assumed he would return to his activities in Fanling, but he believed his much younger deputy Mountain Master had grown into the job and deserved it permanently. So, feeling the gang was in good hands, Uncle had resigned.

He had been back to Fanling many times to see friends and — because his opinions were valued — to meet with the new Mountain Master. Those meetings were frequent during his early years in Kowloon, but gradually diminished as time went by. A trip to Dong's Kitchen was invariably part of any visit.

The weather was pleasant for January, with a moderate temperature, a few clouds, and a light wind. Uncle rarely wore anything except a black suit and a white shirt buttoned to the collar, and on this day it was all he needed to be comfortable. As he walked, he was surprised at how little the street had changed over the years. Among other businesses, the newsstand where he had bought his newspapers and racing forms was still there, but he was surprised to see the old owner standing outside. Uncle thought, or at least had been told, that he had left Fanling several years before.

Ten minutes later, he reached Jia's Congee Restaurant, where he had eaten breakfast virtually every morning of those forty-five years. He peeked inside and saw Jia standing at the rear, talking to a customer. He didn't expect to see her. She had to be at least ninety, and though she had always sworn that she would never retire, he thought her work would have taken its toll. Still, she seemed to be keeping at it, and truthfully, she didn't look like she was anything close to that age. He considered saying hello, but she seemed busy with her customer, so he turned away and continued walking.

Instead of going left, which would have taken him towards the gang's administrative offices, Uncle went right and was soon in an area of town which wasn't familiar to him. He thought he was going in the proper direction, but he had never walked to Dong's this way, so he wasn't completely sure. The street he was on was quiet, with hardly any traffic and only the occasional pedestrian. He tried to stop one to ask if he was headed in the right direction, but the man brushed past him. Uncle began to feel ill at ease. This wasn't an emotion he was accustomed to, particularly when the cause was as trivial as being in a part of Fanling he didn't know. *Pull yourself together. Just keep walking and you are bound to reach Dong's eventually.*

Five minutes turned into ten and then fifteen, and still there was no sight of Dong's. Uncle's unease increased. He began to consider turning around and heading back to his apartment, but he wasn't sure he could find the way. *Could I be dreaming?* he thought as he approached an intersection with a four-way stop. He could go straight, turn right, or turn left. He went straight and started down a steep hill. He hadn't gone more than halfway when a familiar aroma tickled his nose. He took a deep sniff and smiled as he recognized the scent of Dong's secret chicken feet sauce.

At the bottom of the hill there was another four-way intersection, but this time there was no indecision on his part, as Dong's Kitchen came into view across from where he stood. Uncle crossed the street and paused for a few seconds as he wondered why the windows were covered with blinds and the door was closed. Then he heard voices inside and his questions were forgotten. He turned the handle and stepped inside.

PART ONE

(1)
Kowloon, Hong Kong
September 2015

UNCLE HAD FACED THE PROSPECT OF DEATH BEFORE,
but this time was different. He was no longer the young man
living in the Chinese village of Changzhai, trying to survive
the famine triggered by Mao Zedong's Great Leap Forward —
a famine that had taken the lives of his entire family and countless friends. He wasn't standing at two a.m. on the Chinese
side of Shenzhen Bay looking across four kilometres of dark,
dangerous water at the flickering lights of Yuen Long, wondering if he, his fiancée, and his friends would survive the swim to
freedom. He wasn't the newly initiated forty-niner stepping in
front of his Mountain Master as a brother from another gang
ran at them wielding a knife. He wasn't the Fanling Mountain
Master who on two occasions faced down rival gang members
trying to hack him to pieces with machetes. He wasn't on his
knees in a Chinese prison with a gun being held to his head
as a PLA officer pulled the trigger on five empty chambers and
told him to get ready to meet his ancestors as he prepared to
fire the sixth. This time was like none of those.

Uncle was sitting in the office of Doctor Graham Parker in a building located a few blocks from the Queen Elizabeth Hospital in Kowloon. Parker was an oncologist who Uncle had been quietly referred to by his family doctor. Doctor Cho had first recommended that Uncle see a Chinese specialist, but Uncle had demurred. Always a private man, the fact he could be seriously ill wasn't something he wanted known, and the chance that a Chinese doctor might let it slip was something he didn't want to risk. So Cho had referred him to Parker, but not before discussing Uncle's wish for privacy and getting assurances from Parker that things would be handled properly. Parker had not disappointed.

On his first visit two weeks previous, Uncle had detailed his symptoms. Parker had made notes as he spoke about heartburn, indigestion, stomach pain, and nausea. When he mentioned nausea, Parker looked up.

"Have you been throwing up frequently?"

"Yes. It used to be just once in a while, but then it started happening every time I ate anything spicy," said Uncle. "It has gotten better since I began eating blander food."

"And when you throw up, is there ever blood with the food?"

"Yes."

Parker nodded, and Uncle thought he detected a hint of resignation.

"Have you had any trouble swallowing?" Parker continued.

"Sometimes, and there are days when I lose my appetite completely."

"Have you lost weight?"

"I don't know. I never weigh myself," said Uncle.

"That's not important. Your other symptoms tell their own

story," said Parker. "I have to tell you that Doctor Cho suspects you have stomach cancer, which is why he sent you to me."

"I am aware that's what he thinks. It has been difficult for me not to draw the same conclusion."

Parker looked at the file in front of him. "According to your file you have never been seriously ill before now."

"That's true. I might have had the occasional cold or flu bug, but nothing more than that."

"It also says here that you smoke."

"I do. Doctor Cho has been haranguing me for years to quit, but I never listened to him. Are you going to tell me the same thing?"

"No," said Parker. "Short-term smoking is not going to cause any additional damage, but quitting could put extra stress on your system, and until we finalize a diagnosis there's nothing positive to be gained."

"If I have stomach cancer, Cho said smoking could have been a cause."

"Indeed, but first we have to determine what exactly is the problem — and if it is what Doctor Cho suspects, what stage it's at," Parker said. "We need to run some tests. What is your availability?"

"I have no plans past this meeting."

"Then I will schedule an endoscopy and a scan, and depending on what they reveal, we'll do some biopsies," Parker said. "Do you know what an endoscopy is?"

"No."

"Do you want to know? I only ask because I have some patients who prefer not knowing anything."

"I'm the opposite. I would like you to be totally honest with me about everything."

"Good, I prefer that," said Parker. "An endoscopy is a procedure that allows us to see what's going on in your upper digestive tract. A long, flexible tube with a tiny camera attached to the end will be passed down your throat and we'll take pictures."

"And the biopsies?"

"If I don't like what the pictures show, I'll bring you back to the clinic for those."

"Will I be hospitalized for this?" Uncle asked.

"No, that's not necessary. There is an outpatient clinic on the ground floor of this building which is very competent. I use it all the time. The only problem is that they are busy, so it may take a day or two to get you an appointment."

"Like I said, I am available whenever you need me."

As it was, the day or two had turned into a week, and after the various tests, Parker had asked Uncle to return to the clinic for biopsies. This trip to the doctor's office was to get those results, and despite his outward bravado, Uncle was anxious as he sat in the waiting room.

"Mr. Chow, Doctor Parker is ready for you now," the nurse said.

He followed her into Parker's office, took a seat, and looked at Parker across the desk.

The doctor glanced up, hesitated, and then returned to what he was reading.

"Are those my biopsy results?" Uncle asked.

"Yes," Parker said. Then he closed the file and leaned back in his chair. "They aren't what I'd hoped for."

"How bad is it?"

"You have cancer, as we suspected, and unfortunately it is metastatic. It has invaded your lymph nodes and is attacking your lungs and other organs."

Uncle felt a cold chill and struggled not to tremble. "That sounds very bad."

"It is."

"Is it curable? Can it be contained? Will surgery help?"

Parker sat forward, put his hands together on the desk, and shook his head. "I don't think surgery is a realistic option right now, but there are treatments we can employ. If they work, then we can revisit the subject of surgery later," he said. "But, being totally honest with you, we can't avoid the fact that the cancer is pervasive."

"That doesn't answer my question."

"I thought it did. To be blunter, I could tell you there is hope, but truthfully I think the best we can do is contain it for as long as we can. Without a miracle of some sort, it is going to kill you. The question we can't answer is when. The treatments could extend your life by months, and maybe even a year or two. Right now, that's the best I can offer."

"I know I asked you to be honest, but you didn't have to go overboard," Uncle said, and then when he saw Parker's face stiffen, he smiled. "That was a joke, doctor."

"You have a strange sense of humour, Mr. Chow," Parker said.

"If I wail and moan and throw myself on the floor, will that make things any better?"

"Of course not."

"Then why not make a little joke instead?"

"I admire your attitude," Parker said.

"Thank you. Now please tell me about the treatments and how soon I can start them."

"I would like to begin with chemotherapy, which involves taking a series of drugs designed to kill the cancer cells. At this point that's our best bet for extending your life," the doctor said. "If it works and we can isolate the tumours, then we could switch to surgery or radiation therapy to go after them as more specific targets."

"Will I have to be hospitalized?"

"No, you will be a day patient at the Queen Elizabeth, unless there are some unforeseen complications. But I have to warn you that there will be side effects. The drugs can be debilitating. You could suffer hair loss, feel fatigued, and have severe nausea and vomiting. You would also be more susceptible to infection."

"I'm experiencing most of those symptoms now."

"This could be to a stronger degree. Do you have someone who can drive you to the hospital?"

Uncle did, but he wasn't about to use him. Sonny Kwok had been his bodyguard and driver for twenty years, but the two men kept their personal lives out of their relationship. Uncle knew virtually nothing about what Sonny did when he wasn't working for him, and the same was true in reverse. "I'll figure that out," he said. "I'm sure I won't be so weak that I can't take a taxi."

"Everyone reacts a little differently to the treatments. But in case you react badly, do you have someone who can help you at home?"

"I have a housekeeper," said Uncle.

"Good, does she live in?"

"Yes."

"Even better."

"When can the treatments start?" Uncle asked.

"I'll have my assistant book some sessions. Unfortunately, demand is high right now, so I don't expect we'll be able to start until next week at the earliest. Someone from my office will contact you when we have dates."

"I'll wait to hear from them," Uncle said, rising from the chair.

"Before you go," Parker said as he stood, "Doctor Cho explained your desire to keep this situation private. I would like you to know that my office will do everything it can to honour your wishes."

"Thank you," said Uncle.

When he reached the sidewalk, Uncle decided to walk to his apartment on Kwun Chung Street. What had been a hot and humid summer was finally easing, and they had entered what was usually a short window of pleasant weather before the onset of a cold and wet winter. *Days like this shouldn't be wasted.*

Uncle wasn't surprised by Parker's findings. Cho had made his suspicions clear. His stomach had been acting up for more than a year, and he had ignored it until a few months before, when after a dinner with his friend Fong, he had thrown up. The vomit was streaked with blood. It had alarmed Fong, and truthfully — although he had downplayed it — Uncle was alarmed as well. Still, thinking it was a one-off thing, he had delayed going to see Cho. Then a month or so later he'd thrown up again, with the same result. Now he chided himself for letting it get to that point. *Well, what's done is done*, he thought. There was no going back, and as difficult as going forward might be, there was no other choice, so he needed to figure out how best to handle it.

2

UNCLE'S DESIRE FOR PRIVACY WASN'T JUST RELATED TO the cancer. It was the way he had conducted his life since the death of his fiancée, Lin Gui-San. He had felt so much guilt and pain over how she had died during the swim across Shenzhen Bay that his body had ached for months, and there were times he thought his head was going to explode. He had survived by putting his emotions into a compartment that was separate from the world around him. As long as he kept them apart, he could function. What he believed he couldn't withstand was opening the compartment. It was his secret chamber — the place where he hid his fears.

This left him with several challenges. How was he going to explain to Sonny why he didn't want his services on treatment days? Sonny was totally devoted to Uncle and made himself available twenty-four hours a day, seven days a week. In fact, Uncle couldn't remember a week when Sonny hadn't driven him or performed numerous errands. If Uncle was out of touch, if he was unreachable, Sonny would worry. He might even be concerned enough to try to find out why. Uncle needed to concoct an excuse, but none came readily to mind.

Then there was Lourdes. Uncle had never thought that he needed a housekeeper, but then one day, eight years before, Lourdes had shown up at his door. She was Filipina and had been working on contract for a family on the floor below Uncle's. They'd moved out of the building with no notice, leaving her suddenly homeless. Devastated, she had gone from door to door asking if anyone needed a housekeeper or nanny. When Uncle opened his door and saw her standing there with an old suitcase and two plastic grocery bags, his heart had gone out to her.

Uncle knew he was probably the only person in the building who had an unoccupied bedroom, and so he had told Lourdes she could stay until she found another employer. Eight years later, she was still there — never officially employed but paid a normal wage. She cleaned the apartment, did the laundry and ironing, cooked meals, and otherwise stayed out of Uncle's way. During the day, she went for walks with some of the other neighbourhood domestics. In the evenings she watched Filipino soap operas and variety shows on the TV in her room. Uncle figured she had never asked him for an official contract because she was afraid he'd say no. And he knew he didn't have the heart to ask her to leave unless she had somewhere else to go.

In a way, having Lourdes in the apartment had been a blessing. During recent bouts of illness, she had been caring and attentive. What he had to ensure was that she said nothing to Sonny or anyone else about his health.

Lastly, and vastly most important, there was his business partner, Ava Lee, to worry about. They had been partners in a debt collection business for ten years, but their relationship went well beyond business. There was no one he trusted more, and despite a fifty-year age gap, their lives had become intertwined. They didn't share everything, and although many parts of their lives were never discussed, there was a mutual understanding about even those things that were left unsaid. Uncle thought of Ava as much as a granddaughter as a partner, and he knew she felt similarly about him. But even though she was the most important person in his life, he wasn't ready to tell her he was ill, and he was also worried about what the future might hold for her.

They had made many millions of dollars together in fees, and he was going to leave her the bulk of his wealth, so money wasn't going to be a concern for her. Still, how would she move forward without him? She wasn't the type of person to be idle, but he sensed the collection business had already taken a large toll on her, and without him, he couldn't see her continuing with it. Her last job, two months before, had been to recover money her half-brother and his business partner had lost in a Macau land swindle. It had started out as a personal matter between Ava and her brother, but Uncle and Ava's friend May Ling Wong had eventually assisted her in reaching a quasi-satisfying conclusion. The satisfying part had been the recovery of the money; the quasi part was that Ava had been shot in the hip, and in turn had shot and killed the swindle's perpetrator. Uncle had seen first-hand her emotional shock after the shootings. She hadn't worked since then, and although they often spoke, there had been no discussion of her taking another job.

What is Ava going to do? he wondered. *And what can I do to help her ease her way into a new future?*

When he reached his apartment building, Uncle

considered buying some San Miguel beer from the Nepalese restaurant on the ground floor, before deciding it might not be the best thing for his stomach.

"Sir, is there anything I can get you?" Lourdes asked as she hurried out of her bedroom when he entered the apartment.

"No, but I need to talk you. Let's sit."

For the first few months that Lourdes was with him, he had tried unsuccessfully to get her to call him Uncle. She would nod and then continue to call him "sir." He eventually gave up.

Before Lourdes's arrival, his living room furniture had consisted of a red leather chair, two folding trays, and a television. He had since bought a small, round dining table that came with four chairs, as well as a black leather couch and a coffee table. Uncle sat at the dining table now, and she joined him.

"Did anyone call while I was out?" he asked.

"Ava did. She said she'd call back in a little while."

"How did she sound?"

"The same as always," said Lourdes.

When Uncle looked across the table at her, she averted her eyes as she usually did. He took a deep breath and then adopted his "boss" tone. "I want you to listen carefully to me, because I don't want there to be any misunderstanding about this," he began.

"Yes, sir," she said, a touch of panic evident.

"Everything I am about to say has to stay strictly between us. You can't whisper a word of it to Sonny, Ava, Uncle Fong, any of my other friends, or any of the nannies you spend your Sundays with in Statue Square."

"I won't say anything, sir."

"Okay, well, the thing is, I have a medical problem that is going to require some treatment," he said. "It isn't anything major and won't even require any hospitalization, so it is nothing to fret about. But the doctor tells me there might be a few mild side effects. For example, I could be more tired than usual and my appetite may not be as strong. This could go on for three or four weeks, so it's possible that Sonny and some of the others could start asking questions. If they do, all I want you to say is that I'm looking and feeling fine."

She glanced at him, and he saw concern in her eyes. "But what if you aren't fine?" she asked.

"If I'm not, it will only be temporary, and I want you to still tell them that I am. I don't want any unnecessary worry or fussing when there is absolutely no reason for it."

"I can do that, sir," she said.

Uncle heard the words but wasn't sure he heard any conviction. "Lourdes, I have never been more serious. You must do exactly as I say. Don't disappoint me," he said firmly.

She shook her head. "I would never dare go against your word."

"Good," he said, and then was interrupted by the phone. He left the table and picked it up. "*Wei.*"

"Uncle, it's me," Ava said.

"Is everything okay?" he asked.

"I was going to ask you the same question."

"I'm fine. It is just that you usually don't call this late unless there is something pressing."

"Sorry if I alarmed you," she said. "We've been offered a sort of a job, and I wanted to discuss it with you and get your opinion."

"What 'sort of a job'?"

"A small one, for a Vietnamese woman who knows my mother. She and her family are out of pocket about three million Canadian dollars."

He hesitated. They had stopped taking on jobs of that size, but Ava sounded eager, so he said, "Tell me the details."

"The woman's name is Theresa Ng. From what I've been told, her family and other Vietnamese-Canadian families put money into an investment fund called Emerald Lion that sounds like it was a Ponzi scheme. The fund has disappeared, and the guy who ran it took off, although they think they've located him in Ho Chi Minh City."

"You said her family's loss was about three million?"

"Yes."

"What about the other families? How much did they lose?"

"Theresa's not sure, but she thinks it could be anywhere from twenty-five to forty million."

Uncle paused again. *Does Ava really want to pursue this? There's one way to find out*, he thought. "Recovering thirty million dollars interests me," he said.

"Uncle, Theresa has lost three million, not thirty."

"I know, but all those other people who lost money — you do not think they want it back?"

"I'm sure they do, but they haven't approached us."

"Maybe because they don't know who we are."

"Uncle, I'm not about to start chasing down these people one by one to ask them to hire us."

"But there is nothing to stop Theresa Ng from contacting them, is there? Let her do the work. Tell her to get hold of them and persuade them to sign on with us. Organize a meeting if she has to. Three million is of no interest, but if she can deliver commitments for anything more than twenty, then let us take the job," he said.

He heard Ava sigh, and smiled. Ava's sighs rarely resulted in her opposing his requests.

"Okay," she finally said. "I'll call Theresa and see if she is willing to do this. If she is, I'll give her a week to pull it together. How does that sound?"

"That sounds reasonable."

Ava hesitated and then said, "Before I go, can I change the subject to something more personal?"

"Yes, of course," Uncle said with more certainty than he felt.

"When I spoke to Lourdes earlier today, she mentioned you were still having some stomach issues."

Uncle turned to glare at the housekeeper. "I had a slight touch of food poisoning. I have to stop eating bargain sashimi."

"You have enough money to buy the most expensive sashimi in Tokyo a thousand times a day."

"Old habits die hard. You know I can't resist a bargain."

"My mother says, 'penny wise, pound foolish.'"

"You mother knows a lot of clichés."

"That doesn't mean it isn't true."

"I promise, I will be more careful," he said. "Call me after you've spoken to Theresa."

He hung up the phone. "Ava just told me you were discussing my health with her earlier," he said to Lourdes.

Lourdes lowered her head. "She cares for you so much and is always asking how you are. I felt I had to say something, and you hadn't told me yet to say nothing. But now I know better. Not another word, I promise."

"Fine," Uncle said, although he couldn't help thinking that it was going to be harder to keep his health issues private than he had imagined.

After Lourdes went into her bedroom, Uncle picked up *Sing Tao* and the *Oriental Daily News*. He had bought the papers on the walk home from the doctor's office, and now he settled into his red leather chair to read them. He opened the *Daily News* first and turned directly to the sports section. The arrival of September had ended the summer hiatus of Hong Kong horse racing, and races were being run again on Wednesday evenings at Happy Valley and on Sunday afternoons at Sha Tin. Betting on horse racing was Uncle's only hobby, and in addition to the four to five hours he spent at the tracks on race days, he spent many more hours studying the form and handicapping. The *Daily News* had a particularly good racing writer, and Uncle was keen to see his analysis of the races that had been run the day before in Sha Tin.

Uncle read and agreed with his comments on the first race, and had just started on the second when his phone rang. For a second he thought it might be Ava calling back, but then he looked at the screen and saw a Hong Kong number he didn't recognize.

"*Wei*," he answered.

"Mr. Chow, this is Dr. Graham Parker calling. Is this a good time to chat?"

"Of course, but I didn't expect to hear from you so quickly," Uncle said, hiding his surprise.

"Well, as it turned out, I had the occasion to speak to a colleague who helps manage the outpatient clinic I mentioned earlier today. We discussed your case, and when

I stressed to her that I wanted to start your treatments as soon as possible, she told me that one of her patients had backed out of his session at the last minute, so she has an immediate opening," Parker said. "The only problem is that the first session would be tomorrow morning. Is that too much of a rush for you?"

"Since waiting is only going to worsen my situation, there is no such thing as 'too much of a rush.'"

"Excellent, then we will start tomorrow," Parker said. "I have scheduled two sessions, for tomorrow and the day after. The second day is more than I'd usually prescribe, but I believe we should start as aggressively as possible. After that, we'll take a week's break to give you a chance to recover, and then repeat the cycle. I won't lie to you, this will be a heavy dose of chemo, but as you say, given your situation there is no point in being tentative."

"I am not a doctor, and it would be foolish of me not to trust your judgement. Where am I going and what time should I be there?"

"The cancer outpatient clinic is on the ground floor of R Block at the Queen Elizabeth. Your session is scheduled for ten, but you should be there for nine-thirty to register and receive a briefing."

"A briefing?"

"My colleague, Doctor Ma, speaks to everyone who's about to undergo chemotherapy. Knowing what to expect should make things easier."

"I am very much in favour of easier," Uncle said. "Will I see you there?"

"Not when you arrive, but I'll drop in later to check on you."

"How long will this treatment take?"

"Like I said, we're going to give you a heavy dose of chemotherapy, so don't make any other plans for the day," said Parker. "And one more thing: do not eat anything tomorrow morning, and if you have to drink, drink water."

"Is there anything else I need to know?"

"Yes, it could be a long day. There is a television in the clinic, but you might want to bring a book or your own audio device."

"I trust no one would object to me working on the racing form?" asked Uncle.

Parker laughed. "Of course not, although you'll probably be asked for tips."

3

UNCLE DID NOT SLEEP WELL THAT NIGHT. DURING THE day, he hadn't thought much about the consequences of his diagnosis, but as he lay in the dark his mind fixated, and the fact that his death seemed to be in clear sight sent a chill through his bones. He had never been afraid of death, and he had been calm, almost fatalistic, on those occasions when he had encountered the possibility that his days were nearly done. But those had mainly been spur-of-the-moment reactions. There hadn't been the time to really think about consequences. Now his head was full of nothing else, and what made it worse was the lack of certainty. When, where, how would the end come to pass?

Since fleeing China, Uncle had controlled the life he led. Now he felt he had lost that control. Or had he? He still had the option of foregoing the treatment and accepting the outcome. But how sensible was that? And how contrary was that to another of his basic traits — his refusal to be passive when confronted with challenges? He would fight this thing, he decided. He would fight it as hard and for as long as he could. If he reached a point where fighting it came into conflict with his common sense, then that was the time he'd concede. Until then, he'd give it all he had, because every extra day was time he could use to make the future more secure for the people who mattered to him.

Uncle climbed out of bed just after six. He started to make a cup of coffee before remembering Parker's instruction to stick to water. One cup wouldn't hurt, he thought, and then he chided himself. If he was going to do this, he should do it properly. He poured a glass of water, lit a Marlboro, and sat in his chair to watch Kwun Chung Street come to life.

Just before seven, he went into the bathroom to shower and shave. Then, dressed in a black suit and white shirt buttoned to the collar, he left the apartment. He bought *Sing Tao*, the *Oriental Daily News*, and the racing form for Happy Valley, and continued on to the Morning Blessings Restaurant. He wasn't going to eat, but he felt a need to be around familiar faces and surroundings.

The owner, Suki, sat him as soon as he arrived, and before she could say anything, he spoke: "I have blood work later this morning and I have to fast for it so I won't be eating anything, and the only thing I can drink is water." He took two HK hundred-dollar bills from his wallet. "This is what I usually spend, and I insist that you take it. In fact, I would be offended if you didn't, since I'm occupying a table that would otherwise be generating revenue for you."

Suki shook her head. "You don't have to do that," she said.

"I do. Please take the money or I will have to leave."

She grimaced but took the bills. "Can you at least have hot water?"

"I think that will be fine."

"With a slice of lemon?"

"To be on the safe side, I'd better not."

When Suki left, Uncle spread the *Daily News* in front of him. As always, it was heavy with news from and about China. Li Ka-shing, the wealthiest man in Hong Kong, was pulling investments out of the mainland. The article wondered whether he was doing it for political or business reasons, which Uncle thought was a naive question, since in his experience politics and business were almost impossible to separate in China. Less obtuse was a story about the People's Liberation Army's commitment to remodel part of its forces along American lines. Uncle didn't doubt that was true, and he assumed it had been announced to send a message to the Americans that the Chinese were catching up to them militarily. The last story that caught his attention involved a Chinese-American scientist who had been arrested at his home in Philadelphia and charged with spying. Born in China, and now an American citizen, the man represented the conundrum of divided loyalties that was in constant play in Hong Kong, and which the Chinese government was only too pleased to exploit.

Uncle sipped water as he read, conscious of his craving for caffeine. He compensated by smoking more than usual. It wasn't until he replaced the *Daily News* with *Sing Tao* — Sonny's favourite newspaper — that Uncle suddenly remembered he hadn't told his driver that he wouldn't need him for the next few days. He called Sonny's mobile phone, hoping to catch him before he left his apartment.

"Uncle, I was just leaving. Are you at Morning Blessings?" Sonny answered, slightly out of breath.

"Yes, I am, but there's no reason for you to come here. Apologies, I should have called you last night, but I was preoccupied," said Uncle, carefully choosing his words. "I have some personal business to take care of over the next few days and I won't need you to drive me. So take some time off. I'll call you when things are settled."

"A few days…like two or three?" Sonny asked.

"Yes, that should be about right," said Uncle, ignoring the curiosity in Sonny's voice.

There was a long pause before Sonny continued. "Uncle, is everything okay? I don't mean to pry, but this isn't like you."

"You may not mean to pry, but that is exactly what you are doing," Uncle said. "I have some personal business to attend to. What else do you need to know?"

"Nothing."

"Good, and I apologize again for not telling you until the last minute," Uncle said, ending the conversation.

He poured hot water from a pot into his glass and returned to *Sing Tao*. It ran stories about some of the same subjects as the *Daily News* did, but they were written differently, and Uncle read them in full to kill some time. At nine o'clock, he left the restaurant with the racing form tucked under his arm, to walk to the Queen Elizabeth Hospital on Gascoigne Road.

The hospital was a cluster of buildings surrounding the original thirteen-storey structure. They were all well-signed, and Uncle had no difficulty finding R Block. He went through the main entrance and followed the signs to the cancer clinic. There was a lineup at the registration desk and Uncle joined it. It moved briskly, and after giving his information to the nurse at the desk he was directed to go to a small room to wait for Doctor Ma.

Uncle was surprised when two women entered the room.

One was middle-aged and wore a nurse's uniform; the other was younger, dressed in a white coat, and wore no makeup. With a fresh face and her hair pinned at the back, she reminded him of Ava.

"Mr. Chow, I am Doctor Ma," the younger woman said.

"Thank you for fitting me in so quickly."

"Doctor Parker's phone call couldn't have come at a better time for you."

"So he said."

She nodded. "Doctor Parker told me you haven't gone through anything like this before."

"That's true."

"And he outlined the recommended treatment cycle to you?"

"He did."

"Then we can get started. This is Nurse Pan. When we go into the main room, she'll be hooking you up to an IV. There will be slight discomfort, but nothing excessive," she said. "Before you leave this room, you should remove your jacket and shirt, and put on a medical gown."

"That's fine," Uncle said.

"I have scheduled a two-hour session for you this morning, followed by an hour's break, and then two more hours of treatment. You will be sitting in a chair which is quite comfortable, and often the biggest problem our patients face is boredom."

"I brought something to work on," Uncle said, pointing to the racing form.

"Excellent, that is my father's favourite type of reading as well," Ma said with a smile. "Now, I know Doctor Parker explained to you some of the possible side effects of the treatment, but I always like to review them with the patient before we begin. Are you okay with that?"

"Of course."

She nodded again. "Chemotherapy doesn't affect everyone in the same way or at the same rate, so these are generalizations. The most immediate effects, and they could occur in a matter of hours, are diarrhea and nausea. Did you eat this morning?"

"No, and I drank only water."

"That's good," she said. "In a few days, you could also start to feel a strong sense of fatigue. Don't fight it. Take as much rest as you need. This could be accompanied by something we call 'chemo brain' — a general sluggishness of your thought processes, sort of like a mental fog. It doesn't happen to everyone, but if you experience it, know that it will pass."

"Okay."

"Then, over a longer term, maybe two weeks from now, you could start to lose some hair, and you might experience weight loss simply because of the nausea and lack of appetite."

"I don't care about my hair," Uncle said, rubbing the back of his buzz cut. "But I don't have so much weight that I can afford to lose it."

"Avoiding spicy food and drinking a lot of water will help."

"What about beer?" Uncle asked with a smile.

"I wouldn't recommend it," Ma said without a return smile. "Now, do you have any questions?"

"Not at this moment."

"Then let's get started."

4

AT JUST AFTER FOUR O'CLOCK, UNCLE LEFT R BLOCK
and headed towards a taxi stand. Any idea he'd had about
walking home had been obliterated two hours before, when
the knots in his stomach started to fray. He had thrown up
and then dry-heaved for ten minutes. When he had settled
into the chair again, his bowels had begun to rebel. He had
twice barely made it to the bathroom, and now all he wanted
to do was get to his apartment without any kind of incident.

As the taxi negotiated its way through Kowloon, Uncle
clenched his teeth in anger at himself for not having taken
the treatment and its aftermath seriously enough. Why had
he thought he would be impervious to after-effects? Why
hadn't he understood what was entailed? *Maybe I've been in
denial*, he thought. *Well, if that's so, this was a wake-up call.*

When they reached the apartment, Uncle paid the driver,
jumped out of the car, and raced upstairs. He managed to
make it to the bathroom before his bowels emptied what
little was left in them.

Lourdes came out of her room as Uncle emerged from
the bathroom.

"Are you okay? You look ill," she said.

"I ate something that didn't agree with me," he said. "I'm going to lie down, and I don't want to be disturbed."

He didn't sleep, but he felt more stable lying down than he had on his feet. He wasn't sure how long he lay there. He knew it was a few hours, because daylight turned into night. Beyond that he had no sense of time. The house phone rang twice, and he heard Lourdes answer. What she said and to whom was a mystery.

Finally, his stomach began to leave him in peace. As it did, his head cleared, and he became more aware of his surroundings. He lifted himself up and sat on the side of the bed without any negative effects. He stayed there for a few minutes, breathing deeply and trying to gather himself. He wobbled a little when he stood, but eventually steadied. He took a few tentative steps forward, and when that went well, he left the bedroom.

Lourdes came out of her room as soon as she heard him. "Is everything okay, sir?" she asked.

"Just fine."

"Can I get you something to eat? I have stir-fried noodles with pork I made earlier."

"No, I think I should let my stomach settle," he said. "I heard the phone ringing. Who called?"

"A Doctor Parker, and Ava."

"What did the doctor want?" Uncle asked, hoping that Parker understood his commitment to privacy extended to Lourdes.

"I don't know. When I told him you were in bed, he just asked me to tell you to call him back when you were able. He said he'd be up late."

"And Ava?"

"She wants you to call her back as well. It sounded important."

"I'll call them from downstairs. I could use some fresh air," he said. He put on his jacket and picked up his mobile phone. He reached into his jacket pocket, confirmed he had Parker's card with his phone numbers, and then left the apartment.

He walked carefully down the stairs and onto the street. It wasn't as busy as it normally was at night, but when Uncle turned on his phone he saw why. It was already past eleven o'clock. He'd had no idea he was in bed that long. Despite the message Parker had left, Uncle was hesitant about calling him so late, but then again Parker might think it was rude if he didn't. Uncle walked past the Nepalese restaurant, found a wall to lean against, and dialled Parker's cell phone number.

"Mr. Chow, I was hoping you would call," Parker answered. "I wanted to apologize for not seeing you at the hospital this afternoon. I had an emergency that required my attention."

"I understand. No apologies are necessary."

"And I'm also wondering how you're feeling? Doctor Ma informed me that you reacted quite severely to the chemo. Unfortunately, we have no way of predicting how it will impact any one individual."

"I am starting to feel human again, but I haven't had anything to drink or eat. I'm almost afraid to," said Uncle.

"You need to stay hydrated, so you should be drinking water. As for food, I would suggest plain white rice for now," Parker said.

"I'll give it a try."

"One other thing I wanted to ask was whether or not you still feel up to a second session tomorrow," said Parker. "We know the treatment is especially effective for attacking cancers when we schedule them close together like that, but it isn't something you should feel compelled to do. We can always push it back a few days."

"Part of me wants to put it off, but that would be avoiding the reality of my situation. So I will go with what's most effective, and hope my reaction tomorrow isn't so intense."

"That's not only a brave choice, but a wise one," said Parker. "And I promise I'll drop in and see you during the day tomorrow."

Uncle ended the call feeling neither particularly brave nor wise; just someone who had been forced to choose the worse of two evils.

"Uncle, are you all right?" a voice said.

He turned and saw Anjay, the owner of the Nepalese restaurant.

"Yes, I'm fine. I just needed some air, although come to think of it I could also use some water. Could you bring me a bottle, please?"

"No beer tonight?" Anjay asked.

"I'm taking a break from beer."

"I'll be right back," said Anjay.

Uncle suddenly felt tired again. He closed his eyes and pressed his head against the wall. However much sleep he'd had, it obviously wasn't enough.

"Here's your water," Anjay said a moment later.

Uncle took it and handed him an HK ten-dollar bill. He saw Anjay was reluctant to take it but forced it into his hand. "We have our agreement that I pay for what I eat and drink.

Let's not start changing our relationship," he said.

When Anjay left, Uncle unscrewed the bottle cap and sipped. When he didn't feel any overt discomfort, he sipped again, and swirled the water around in his mouth before swallowing it. Feeling a little refreshed, he called Ava.

"Uncle?" she answered.

He realized he didn't know when she had called, and because he was typically prompt at getting back to her, she might have worried about the time lag. "I'm sorry for not calling back sooner. I fell asleep, and Lourdes didn't wake me as she should have."

"*Momentai*, it was just that I had news I wanted to share."

"You sound happy."

"We have a job. In addition to Theresa Ng, we now have sixteen clients who've lost a combined thirty-two million Canadian dollars."

"How did that happen so quickly?"

"It was all Theresa. She went into action the moment I told her our conditions. By mid-afternoon yesterday she had contacted everyone she knew who'd lost money, and she made arrangements for a meeting. I went there last night with a stack of our standard contracts and explained in detail how we operate. I thought some of them might be turned off, but they weren't. I have seventeen signed contracts."

"Good, good. It will be nice to be back at work again. I was beginning to wonder if you were ready to retire before me."

"Never," she said.

"So, when do we start?"

"Right away. I have things I need to do here tomorrow. And I have a Vietnamese licence plate number that I hope you can track for me."

He took a pen from his jacket pocket and turned Parker's card to the blank side. "Give it to me," he said.

She read the number and then asked, "How are our contacts in Ho Chi Minh City?"

"Excellent."

"So tracking the plate shouldn't take too long?"

"One phone call, perhaps two, that's all."

"And if I need to go to Vietnam?"

"You will have all the help you need. We have some old colleagues there who are still active, and they have friends in both the police and the army."

"Then, in addition to the licence plate, could you ask them to come up with whatever they can on a Lam Van Dinh? He's at the centre of the scam. He was living in Canada but left when it became obvious the money was missing. He was spotted getting out of a car with those plates about a week ago in Ho Chi Minh, so there must be a record of him entering the country sometime in the past six months. He would have to put his local address on the customs form. It could be entirely bogus, of course, but you never know."

"I will look after it."

"Thanks."

Uncle hesitated, then said slowly, "Ava, I was really worried that you might have had enough of our life. After Macau, I wouldn't have blamed you if you had decided to make a change."

"Truthfully, I did think about it, and May Ling has raised the subject of starting a business together, but I'm not ready to give up what we have," she replied.

Uncle felt the urge to say more, perhaps even gently encourage the idea of her joining forces with May Ling.

Instead, he simply said, "I am glad you gave it some thought. Now, I will contact one of my colleagues in Vietnam, and I'll call you back as soon as I have the information."

The number for his Vietnamese contact was in the apartment, but Uncle didn't leave the wall right away. He thought about the conversation with Ava. It had been awkward, mainly because he had handled it badly. Part of him wanted to confide in her, but he knew she was still recovering from the trauma of Macau, and he didn't want to add to her emotional burden. Besides, he told himself, he had just started chemo, and until it was over he wouldn't really know how things stood. His decision to keep things as private as possible was the right one, even where Ava was concerned.

He left the street and started to climb the stairs to his apartment. Ava was still on his mind, though, and he decided a discreet phone call to May Ling in the next few days might be appropriate.

The door to Lourdes's room was closed, and the apartment was quiet when he entered. He took a small black notebook from a kitchen drawer, found the number for Phan in Ho Chi Minh, and then sat in his chair to make the call.

Phan was only one of several contacts Uncle had in Vietnam, but he was the most senior and had been a strong supporter of Uncle during his tenure as chairman of the triad societies. Uncle knew it was late to call, but he also knew Ho Chi Minh City was one hour behind Hong Kong, and hoped Phan was still up.

"*Ah-lo*," a woman's voice answered.

"Is my old friend Phan still awake? If he is, could you tell him that Uncle is calling from Hong Kong," Uncle said in

Mandarin, a language that he knew Phan — and many other Vietnamese — spoke.

"Wait, I will tell him," she said.

A moment later, Uncle heard Phan's distinctive gravelly voice say, "Is this really Uncle?"

"It is."

"It has been a few years since we last spoke, so I'm sure this isn't a social call. Has some calamity come over you?"

"Not at all, I was just lonely and wanted to hear a friendly voice," Uncle said.

"Will you think I'm being rude if I don't believe you?" Phan laughed.

"No, I will think you haven't lost any of your sense."

"Thank you. Now tell me what you want me to do for you."

"I need two pieces of information. I have a licence plate number, and I'd like to know who owns the car it belongs to. Secondly, a man named Lam Van Dinh arrived in Vietnam sometime in the last six months. His flight would have originated in Canada, and there's a good chance he was using a Canadian passport. I would like to know what he declared on his customs form as his local address," said Uncle. "Are both of those requests doable?"

"Of course, give me the plate number," Phan said.

Uncle took out Parker's card and read the number aloud.

"How soon do you want the information?"

"How soon can you get it?" Uncle asked.

"It might take an hour or two, but not much longer."

"I'll stay up until I hear from you," said Uncle. "And a very big thanks."

"You know thanks aren't necessary, but I do like the idea of you owing me a favour."

Except I may not live long enough for you to collect it, Uncle thought before he realized it. "Believe me, I'd like nothing better than being able to repay you," he said.

Uncle put down the phone and then contemplated how best to spend the next couple of hours. On a normal evening, he would be sitting in his chair with a bottle of San Miguel, a pack of cigarettes, and the racing form. San Miguel was out of the question, but Parker had said he could still smoke, and Uncle thought his mind was sharp enough to tackle the form. He lit a Marlboro, took a drag, looked at the cigarette, and tried to remember when he had started smoking. He had been fifteen or sixteen when he had his first, but he didn't have the money to support the habit until he was in his early twenties. Cigarettes were like an old friend, but an old friend who was now contributing to his death. He took one more drag, stubbed it out, and picked up the form.

He had barely started on the third race when his eyes began to close. He got out of the chair, walked around it several times, and retook his seat. Within minutes, his eyes began to close again, and this time he didn't fight it.

The phone was on the table next to him, and the volume was turned up, so when it rang it startled him.

"*Wei*," he answered, his voice sleepy.

"This is Phan."

Uncle checked the time. Less than two hours had elapsed since they'd spoken. "If you have my information, I compliment you on your efficiency," he said.

"I have the information, and although it wasn't that difficult, it has generated interest here."

"How so?"

"The car is registered to Lam Duc Dinh."

"Is he related to my person of interest?"

"Yes, he is his older brother . . . and perhaps the leading neurosurgeon in Vietnam."

"That *is* interesting."

"My contacts thought so," Phan said. "They were curious why I would be asking about a car owned by such a distinguished man."

"What did you tell them?"

"I explained that our main interest was his brother."

"Did they have anything on him?"

"He landed in Ho Chi Minh about five months ago, and he did put his brother's address on the customs entry form as his residence."

"Is he known to them otherwise?"

"He has no criminal record, if that's what you mean. He left Vietnam about twenty years ago and has been coming back every three or four years for short visits."

"Phan, do you have any way of confirming he's actually staying with his brother?"

"It's a bit late in the night for that. We can do something in the morning, but I have to say I'll be surprised if he's not there."

"Well, if he is, I expect that my partner will be heading your way. Can I count on you to provide her with support on the ground?"

"Of course, and I presume the partner you're referring to is Ava Lee?"

"It is. I can't remember if you've met her."

"I haven't, but I have heard a lot about her. She has quite a reputation."

"Pardon? What kind of reputation?"

"All very positive," Phan said quickly. "People usually talk about how smart she is, though I've been told she's as tough as she is clever."

"That's true, but she's still going to need support."

"I promise you she'll have it," Phan said. "And I'll speak to you tomorrow morning after we confirm the brother is at the house."

"I'll be at my home number until about nine. After that, you'll have to call my cell. If I don't answer, just leave a message. If Ava is going to travel to Ho Chi Minh, I'll call you with her travel details."

Uncle put down the phone with a feeling of satisfaction. Despite the fact he had been officially out of the triad brotherhood for more than ten years, Phan had treated him with the respect typically reserved for a Mountain Master. And Ava was going to be pleased at how quickly they'd gathered the information she wanted, he thought as he called her.

"Hi Uncle, did your contact come through?" she answered.

"He did, and here's what he found out," Uncle said, and then related his conversation with Phan.

"That's good news, and if he is still at his brother's house, I'll get to Ho Chi Minh as fast as I can," she said. "In fact, in the hope he is there, I'll hold a seat on the Cathay Pacific flight that leaves here at midnight for Hong Kong. I can catch a connection there for Ho Chi Minh."

Even when she was just flying through Hong Kong, Ava and Uncle would try to find a way to meet. He should keep things as normal as possible, he thought. He calculated she would be arriving early in the morning on the day after his next treatment. "As I remember, that flight will get you into

Hong Kong in time for breakfast. If your connection makes it possible, perhaps we could meet for congee?"

"I would like that," she said.

"Okay, I'll call you as soon as I hear from Phan tomorrow, and then we can finalize our plans."

He put down the phone, and then smiled when he thought of Phan's remark about Ava having quite a reputation. It was true, and she had earned it. What was more amazing was that no matter what senior triads knew of her exploits, they were even more impressed when they met her. At five foot three inches, and weighing about one hundred and fifteen pounds, she looked like a strong wind could blow her over when in fact she could take down men twice her size.

Uncle remembered the first time he saw what she was capable of. It had been ten years ago, he realized, almost shocked how those years had flown by. Uncle had just started his debt collection business, and his men Carlo and Andy were in Shenzhen hunting down a thief named Johnny Kung. They had located the hotel he was staying in and had called Uncle with that news, and with one other odd piece of information. Evidently, they weren't the only people going after Kung; there was a young woman, who Andy had referred to as a "girl," chasing him as well. Uncle couldn't imagine why someone would hire a girl, and what made it stranger was that she had come all the way from Canada and didn't seem to have any local support.

At Andy's urging, Uncle had agreed they would work with her, and a plan was concocted that would have her isolate Kung from his bodyguards so Andy and Carlo could get their hands on him. She did her part, but before Andy could get Kung out of the restaurant, one of Kung's bodyguards had arrived on the scene. Uncle's smile broadened as he remembered the phone call he had received from Andy. He had relayed the news that they had Kung, and then mentioned the bodyguard's intrusion.

"How did you handle him?" Uncle had asked.

"Boss, you won't believe this, but it was the girl who took him out. He was waving a gun and she didn't seem to care. She just stepped in front of him and two punches later he was on the ground rolling around in agony. I've never seen anything like it."

At the time, Uncle had thought, *What kind of girl is this?* A few days later he had several answers to that question that included — as Phan had said — the fact she was as smart as she was tough, and as principled as anyone he had ever met. Had she found her way into his heart back then? Perhaps — but with Ava, the longer he knew her the more he came to care for her. Now she was the single most important person in his life.

5

UNCLE WOKE AT SEVEN. HE HAD SLEPT FITFULLY, BUT there had been no mad dashes to the bathroom. It appeared there was nothing left for his body to reject, and for that he was grateful, but he also had a hunger that reminded him of the way he'd felt in China, when starvation had haunted him. He slid out of bed, steadied himself, and then walked into the living room. He went to Lourdes's door and knocked.

A few seconds later, she said, "Yes, sir."

"I'm sorry to bother you so early, but could you make me a bowl of white rice?" he asked.

"What would you like with it?"

"Nothing. A bowl of plain white rice is all I want."

She opened the door slightly and peered at him through the crack. "I'll do it right away."

"Thank you, I'll shower and shave while you get started."

Thirty minutes later he sat at the kitchen table contemplating a mound of white rice. For reasons he understood were psychological and dated back to his escape from China, he always ate quickly — so quickly at times that he barely tasted his food. He knew that wasn't an approach to take with this white rice. He took a few grains on his chopsticks, placed them in his mouth, and let them rest on his tongue. After a few seconds he began to chew as slowly as he could. When he felt the rice's texture turn to mush, he swallowed. He didn't expect his stomach to react immediately, but just in case he waited anyway. When nothing happened, he put a second helping into his mouth and repeated the process. After a few more, his hunger pangs began to recede, and before he was halfway through the bowl, he started to feel full. He put the chopsticks on the table, sipped his water, and sat quietly, willing his stomach not to rebel. After ten minutes, he felt secure enough to stand.

"You can't finish the rice, sir?" Lourdes asked.

Uncle saw her in the doorway of her room and wondered if she had been watching him the whole time. "I've had enough for now. Save what's left; I'll eat it later."

He went into his bedroom, put on a jacket, and returned to the living room to find Lourdes covering the leftover rice. One attribute she shared with him was an inability to waste food.

"I'm going to buy my newspapers," he said. "I will be back."

Uncle felt slightly light-headed as he went down the stairs, but after several deep breaths of fresh air the feeling passed, and he felt comfortable enough to walk to the newsstand. He took his time going there and coming back, conscious of how his body was behaving. When he reached the apartment building, he took up a position near the door. Usually he would have had several cigarettes by now, but for some reason the craving wasn't as strong. He lit his first cigarette of the day and took a drag. The smoke had an unfamiliar bite as it reached his lungs. He took two more drags, had a similar if not quite as strong reaction, and threw the cigarette to the ground.

Uncle checked the time when he entered his apartment and saw he had an hour to spare before leaving for the hospital. He decided to read *Sing Tao* and save the *Oriental Daily News* for later.

"Sir, there were some phone calls," Lourdes said before he got into his chair.

"Did you take messages?"

"Yes, a man named Phan wants you to call him back," she said. "And Sonny was wondering if you had changed your mind about needing him today."

"Thank you," he said, pleased to hear about Phan, but slightly annoyed that Sonny was being so persistent.

He reached for the phone and called Phan.

"I hope you have good news for me," said Uncle as Phan answered.

"I do. Lam is still living at his brother's house."

"How do you know?"

"My nephew Tran went there this morning. He saw him puttering around in the front garden."

"He was sure it was him?"

"Uncle, we have a copy of his passport. He matches the photo."

"Of course," said Uncle. "Well, if that's the case then Ava could be arriving in Ho Chi Minh as early as tomorrow."

"Send me her itinerary when you have it. I'll arrange for her to be met at the airport and escorted through customs. The line-ups there are brutal," said Phan.

"That would be helpful. Who will you send to the airport?"

"Tran. He's an up-and-coming police officer but has ties to the brotherhood. He went to university in Australia and speaks English well. He and Ms. Lee should have no trouble communicating. Tell her he'll be dressed in civilian clothes and will be holding a sign with her name on it."

"Thank you one more time."

"Not a problem, Uncle. We old warriors have to stick together."

Uncle's next call was to Toronto. Ava's line rang five times, and Uncle was becoming concerned he'd missed her when she answered, sounding slightly out of breath.

"I had just stepped out of the shower when I heard the phone," she said. "I had to run to get it."

"I would have left a message."

"Now there's no need. What have you found out?"

"Lam is still in Ho Chi Minh City. Our contacts there saw him in person about an hour ago. He was doing some gardening."

"Then I'll be catching the midnight flight."

"Send me your itinerary before you leave for the airport. I want to let our friends in Ho Chi Minh know when to expect you."

"I'll do that in a few minutes."

"And you might not see me at the airport with Sonny tomorrow morning. I would go with him as usual, but I have a project I've been working on that might need my attention."

"*Momentai*, it will be great just to see you again. These past few months are the longest time we've been apart since we became partners."

"I know, and I have to say I've missed you."

"Me too," said Ava. "Now, I should go. You need the

itinerary and I have to finish packing. I'm rather out of prac-
tice at doing that for an overseas trip."

Uncle put down the phone with a sigh. He hated not telling Ava the entire truth, but until his situation was clarified
that's what he felt he had to do. And speaking of what he had
to do, he phoned Sonny.

"Yes, boss," Sonny answered.

"Lourdes told me you called and asked if I needed you
this morning. Unless I'm being forgetful, I thought I told
you yesterday that I would be tied up for a few days. What
is it you didn't understand?"

There was a long silence, and Uncle knew he had stung
Sonny. It wasn't something he enjoyed doing, but once in a
while it was necessary.

"I'm sorry, boss. I was just checking in."

"Well, you've done that, and nothing has changed where
today is concerned, but tomorrow is different. Ava will be
arriving in Hong Kong on the morning Cathay flight from
Toronto. I'd like you to meet her and then bring her to
Morning Blessings."

"Okay, I'll look after it."

Uncle sat back in his chair and opened *Sing Tao*. It was
Wednesday and that meant night racing at Happy Valley, so
almost automatically he turned to the back pages to see what
the paper's handicapper was choosing. But as he compared the
picks to his own preliminary ones it occurred to him that he
might not be well enough to go. It was a random thought that
caught him off guard. He tried to remember the last time he
had missed a race night at Happy Valley, and couldn't recall
ever missing a single one. The prospect shook him. In terms of
changes in his life, not going to Happy Valley would be major.

Well, he didn't have to make that decision, he thought, until after the day's treatment. Maybe it wouldn't hit him as hard as it had the day before.

At nine-fifteen, he folded *Sing Tao* and prepared to leave for the hospital. Just as he was slipping on his jacket, the phone rang, and he saw Ava's Toronto number.

"Is everything okay?" he asked, surprised to hear from her so soon.

"Yes, I'm in a limo on my way to the airport. I'm booked on a Dragonair flight that will arrive in Ho Chi Minh at three-thirty."

"I'll let our Vietnamese friends know."

"Fine, and I'll see you for breakfast tomorrow in Hong Kong," she said. "You have no idea how enjoyable it is for me to say those words."

6

PARKER DIDN'T COME TO SEE UNCLE AT THE QUEEN Elizabeth until he had started his second treatment of the day. The first had gone well enough; though he felt weak and light-headed, the nausea wasn't as bad as the day before and the diarrhea hadn't returned.

"I hope they're looking after you to your satisfaction," Parker said as he sat down next to Uncle.

"It is all very professional."

"We have a very good team here," Parker said. "How are you holding up today?"

"Better than yesterday."

"There will be ups and downs. The important thing is not to strain yourself even when you feel normal. With this treatment, you can go from fine to awful in a matter of minutes."

Uncle pointed at the racing form. "I was considering going to Happy Valley tonight."

Parker shook his head. "I would advise against it, and that's coming from someone who is no stranger to Happy Valley," he said. "As well behaved as those crowds are, moving amongst them will take a lot of energy, and you don't have much to spare. I suggest you stay home, place your bets with a bookie, and watch the races on television."

"And have plain white rice for dinner," Uncle said with a smile.

"Is that what you had last night?"

"No, I had it for breakfast."

"Have you kept it down?"

"Yes."

"Then stick with it. If you still feel okay tomorrow, you can be a little more adventurous."

"I was going to meet a friend for congee tomorrow morning," said Uncle.

"That should be fine as long as you don't jazz it up with things like spicy sausage, pepper, and soy sauce."

"You seem to know a lot about congee."

"I was born and raised in Hong Kong and had an amah who fed it to me several times a week."

"I'll keep it simple."

"That is very wise of you, but that shouldn't surprise me after the way Doctor Cho described you."

Uncle cocked an eyebrow at Parker. He had expected that when Cho told Parker about Uncle's desire for privacy, some information had been shared about Uncle's roots. He only hoped Cho hadn't gone overboard.

Parker seemed to sense Uncle's discomfort. "He spoke about you only in the most general terms, of course," he added quickly, before getting up to leave.

When Parker was gone, Uncle took out his cell phone. Patients were asked not to use their phones except in cases of family emergency. In Uncle's mind, not going to Happy Valley qualified as one.

"Uncle, great to hear from you," his friend Fong answered.

Unlike Uncle, Fong hadn't retired from the triad life — partially because his gambling hobby kept him in need of regular pay. Among other things, he helped supervise the operation of the Fanling gang's betting shops.

"I need your help with something," said Uncle.

"Name it," Fong replied without hesitation.

"I would like you to open an account in my name at the betting shop in Dong's Kitchen."

There was a longer pause than Uncle had expected, and then Fong said, "Of course. How much credit do you want?"

"Fifty thousand."

"No problem. But, Uncle, if I can ask, why do you need an account at Dong's?"

"I want to bet on the races at Happy Valley tonight."

Fong went quiet, and Uncle imagined what questions were running through his head.

"I have a stomach bug that hits without warning. Doctor Cho has prescribed medicine for it, but he tells me it will take about twenty-four hours to kick in. I don't want to risk embarrassing myself in public, so I'm going to watch the races from home tonight."

"It must be serious if you're going to miss a night at Happy Valley."

"It is."

"Well, get better, Uncle. I'm not used to you being under the weather," said Fong. "And I'll let Dong's know you'll be calling in your bets."

"Thanks, Fong," Uncle said, ending the conversation.

Of all the people still in his life, no one had known him longer — or knew him better — than Fong. As young triads,

Fong, Uncle, and their friend Xu had supported each other without question. Xu's move to Shanghai to set up his own gang had removed him from their immediate orbit, though the trust and affection among them never weakened. That left Fong as Uncle's closest advisor, and there was rarely a day when the two men didn't talk.

If these treatments don't work, Uncle thought, *Fong will be the first person I confide in.* There were things he would need done that he didn't want to ask of Ava or Sonny — things that were rooted in his past, things that Fong understood. None was more important than Lin Gui-San. If he died — *when* he died — provisions would have to be made, and Uncle knew he could trust Fong to carry out his wishes. The same was true of Ava and Sonny, of course, but asking them would require answering questions about a part of his life that he had always kept secret. Fong knew of Lin Gui-San and how she had died. But he didn't yet know about the niche in the Ancestor Worship Hall on Fo Look Hill in Yuen Long that contained her urn. When the time was right, Uncle decided, Fong would have to be told.

In the meantime, Uncle thought, *life can go on, and there are races at Happy Valley that need to be handicapped.*

At four-thirty Uncle left the hospital and headed directly to his apartment. His stomach was still behaving well but fatigue had set in, and his thought processes were decidedly slower. When he got home, he wanted to nap, and he wanted to eat. The question was in which order?

He ate first — a bowl of plain steamed rice accompanied by a glass of water. There were no immediate after-effects, and he felt comfortably full when he lay on the bed. Within minutes he was asleep, and if Lourdes hadn't knocked on his door as arranged at six-thirty, he thought he could have slept the night away.

Post time for the first race was seven-fifteen. Sitting in his chair with the racing form in his lap and the phone by his side, Uncle reviewed his selections and then called Dong's. To his surprise, Fong answered.

"What are you doing taking calls?" Uncle asked.

"I work at the shops now and then. It keeps me in touch," Fong said. "Besides, I couldn't abide the thought of you calling here and running into a problem. So I decided to make sure there weren't any. Now, who are you betting on in the first race?"

Three hours later, Uncle said good night to his friend. When he was at Happy Valley, he usually left after placing his bet on the last race, to avoid the crush of the mass exodus. Sitting at home, there wasn't really a reason not to watch it, but even though he was a practical man, Uncle had several ingrained superstitions when it came to horse racing. Leaving before the last race was one of them. Did it still apply if he wasn't at Happy Valley? He was up fifteen thousand for the evening and had bet it all on the final race. *Why take the chance you'll turn your luck bad*, he thought, as he slid from his chair and turned off the television.

(7)

UNCLE WOKE AT SIX-THIRTY AFTER A FITFUL NIGHT'S
sleep. He lay quietly for a few minutes as he tried to recon-
cile a body that felt lethargic with a mind that was rapidly
turning over. The mind finally prevailed, and he rose from
bed. He went into the living room, checked for messages,
and finding none he went into the bathroom to prepare to
meet Ava for breakfast. If her flight was on time, it would
have landed at six-thirty, but after the taxi to the terminal, debarkation, and a long walk to customs, he figured it
would be at least seven-thirty by the time she met Sonny. It
was a thirty-kilometre drive from the airport to Kowloon,
and at that time of morning it would take more than half
an hour, which meant she would get to Morning Blessings
after eight.

By seven, Uncle was sitting fully dressed in his chair
waiting for Sonny to call. After any prolonged time apart,
he was always filled with a sense of anticipation when he
knew he was going to see Ava again. But this was different, because the anticipation was tinged with a nervousness
that he couldn't trust his body. What if his stomach couldn't

handle the congee? Parker had talked about ups and downs in his physical condition, and the last thing he wanted was to have an episode in front of Ava.

By seven-fifteen, Uncle was getting impatient and phoned Sonny's mobile.

"Good morning, boss," Sonny answered.

"Did her plane arrive on time?"

"It was ten minutes late."

"That's not bad. With any luck you'll get her to Morning Blessings around eight-fifteen. I'm going to head over there now. I'll read my papers until she arrives."

"Do you want her to call you from the car?"

"No, I'd rather welcome her in person," said Uncle and then hung up.

If he felt strong enough, he could extend his walk, and if he didn't, he would just take his time. The newsagent nodded as Uncle approached, and as usual held out the day's *Sing Tao* and *Oriental Daily News*. Uncle paid for them, and rather than tucking them under his arm, he opened the *Daily News* and turned to the racing results. His horse had won the last race at odds of three to one, which meant he had turned a profit of HK$60,000 for the night.

Uncle continued his walk to Morning Blessings at a leisurely pace, greeted the owner, Suki, when he got there, and took a seat in his usual booth. "I'm having company this morning," he said to her. "Ava is going to be joining me."

"It will be nice to see her again. She's such a lovely girl," said Suki.

"Did I ever tell you that we formed our partnership while eating here?"

"No, but I'm really pleased to hear that," she said with

a broad grin. "I assume you'll wait for her to arrive before you order."

"Yes, I'll wait."

Uncle opened the *Daily News* to the racing pages, and then worked his way backwards to the front page. He had started to do the same with *Sing Tao* when he heard Suki say loudly, "*Leng lui*, it is so good to see you."

Uncle looked up from his paper and saw Suki leading Ava to his table. *Leng lui* meant "pretty one," a description that fitted Ava perfectly.

He stood up and reached for her. "As beautiful as ever, my girl, as beautiful as ever."

She kissed him on the forehead. "I'm so happy to see you, Uncle."

"You do not mind us eating here?"

"Of course not. You know I love congee."

Suki hovered, waiting for them to sit. As soon as they had, she asked, "Can I take your orders now?"

"I'm going to have plain congee with a glass of water," Uncle said.

Ava glanced at him. "No sausage, pickled vegetables, or salted eggs?"

He shrugged. "My doctor tells me I should be more careful about what I eat. He preaches moderation in all things."

Ava smiled at Suki. "I'm glad my doctor isn't so fussy. I'll have sausage, chopped spring onion, and of course youtiao with mine. I'll also have black coffee."

Uncle waited for Suki to leave before saying, "I was just telling Suki about our first breakfast here."

"When you shocked me by asking me to become your partner?"

He laughed. "You didn't act shocked at the time, and as I remember I had to work very hard to persuade you."

"I was hesitant because I wasn't sure I was good enough to be your partner. As reassuring as you were, there was also something intimidating about you. I didn't want to be a disappointment."

"That wouldn't have been possible," he said. "I've always believed in my ability to judge people, and I had decided I wanted you in my life. Not to boast, but look how well it has all worked out. Ten years of partnership and friendship."

"Yes, Uncle, partnership and a tremendous friendship. The time has gone by so fast; it certainly doesn't feel like ten years."

Uncle noted the word *tremendous* and felt a jolt of joy that he didn't express, instead replying, "What didn't go quickly was the break you took after Macau. I missed you, and I have been worrying about you."

"I'm sorry if I dawdled all summer. It took weeks for my leg to begin functioning normally, and by then I was at the cottage and feeling lazy. I'm back at work now, so let's put those worries aside."

Uncle looked at her and couldn't help thinking she looked more fragile and vulnerable than he'd ever seen her. "Are you sure you are ready to dive back in?"

"Yes, but I have to tell you that I'm not so sure that going to Ho Chi Minh City will result in anything positive. This could be a short assignment."

"Why do you say that?"

"Before I left Toronto, I met with a man named Joey Lac who was a close friend of Lam. He met with Lam before he left for Vietnam, and according to Lac, Lam was visibly distraught. Lac said he was a straight-up person — someone he doesn't believe is even remotely capable of pulling off a scam like this."

"It is always the ones we never suspect until it is too late," Uncle said.

"Still, Lac did seem to know him well," she said.

"You will find out for yourself soon enough," said Uncle, as Suki arrived with their food.

Uncle forced himself to eat slowly. But there was nothing satisfying about plain rice porridge. Ava, on the other hand, ate with enthusiasm, repeatedly dipping her youtiao into the congee.

When they had finished and their bowls had been removed, Ava took out a notebook. "What arrangements have you made for me in Vietnam?" she asked.

"You'll be met at the airport by a man named Tran. He's a police officer, but will be dressed in civilian clothes. He's been told to give you whatever help you need."

"I'm not sure I'll need a police officer. I'm not anticipating any serious trouble. Lam's an accountant, not a fighter."

"Just be cautious. Remember, his brother is a man of substance, and he is going to have powerful friends."

"I'm not going to do anything rash," said Ava, and then tore a blank page from her notebook. She wrote something on it and passed the page to Uncle. "Do we have contacts in Indonesia?"

"Some, mainly in Jakarta," he said, and then pointed at what she'd written. "What is this 'Bank Linno'?"

"It's headquartered in Surabaya. I have only that one name attached to it, plus a phone number and an email address. Could you look into it?"

"Is this connected to Lam?"

"Very much so."

"I know quite a few Indonesian banks, but I've never heard of this one."

"It was big enough to have a branch in Toronto, and that's where Lam was depositing the money he collected. The strange thing is it shut down shortly after Lam ran into trouble."

"And you think there is a connection?" Uncle asked.

"I don't know what to think. That's why I need to talk to Lam."

Uncle nodded. One trait he and Ava shared was that they didn't leap to conclusions. Slow and steady had always been their style; connecting dots until they got to the end. "I will find out what I can about the bank."

Their conversation dwindled. Uncle thought Ava looked slightly uncomfortable and wondered if he was the cause. Before he could ask, she said, "When we spoke a few days ago, I hope you weren't offended that May Ling had talked to me about the possibility of joining forces."

"Why would I be? I can't go on forever, and partnering with her would be a brilliant move," he said. "Besides, you owe me nothing."

"I owe you everything," Ava said, so sharply that it startled him.

His eyes turned away from the table to look out the window. "Sonny is circling outside. We need to get you to the airport."

8

UNCLE INTERRUPTED HIS WALK BACK TO HIS APARTMENT with a stop at a park about halfway from Morning Blessings. It was late enough in the morning that most of the tai chi and other exercise activities were finished, so Uncle could relax in relative peace. He lit a cigarette, took two drags, then threw it to the ground and stepped on it.

He sat on a bench for half an hour thinking about Ava. He hadn't realized just how much he had missed her during their months apart. Her visit had lifted his spirits, but the moment she left with Sonny, he had felt a depression come over him. How many more times would he see her? How much more time would they spend together? Their interactions would increase now that they had a job to pursue, but how long would it last?

Uncle pulled the piece of paper she'd given him out of his jacket pocket. His contact in Jakarta was a man named Chung. He was not a triad, but he was a jago — a leader of a local gang with loose affiliations to the brotherhood. Chung and Uncle had always gotten along well, but it had been several years since they'd spoken and Uncle had no idea if Chung was even still alive.

When Uncle first met him, Chung had been using the name Chungkiri, which was an Indonesian variation of his Chinese name. When he reverted back to the Chinese original, Uncle asked what had motivated it. To his surprise, Chung became quite agitated.

"In 1967, when Suharto came to power, he instituted what he called his New Order, which — among other atrocities — targeted the ethnic Chinese. We were only about three percent of the population, but according to that prick we controlled seventy percent of the economy, and he referred to us as 'economic animals' and 'opportunistic aliens,'" Chung said. "Suharto passed a law that limited what we could own in local businesses; he tried to wipe out every vestige of Chinese culture — hell, even celebrating Chinese New Year was forbidden — and he banned Chinese names. We had to take Indonesian names. Some of us adapted our Chinese names to fit the law. Others adopted a completely new identity. But time and politics change, and after Suharto was deposed, the law was rolled back, and I reverted to my real name. Not everyone did. For some it was too much trouble, and there were still fears about repercussions. The law may have been removed, but anti-Chinese prejudices were alive and well."

Uncle had listened to Chung's story with great interest, and although it might have been an extreme example of the xenophobia aimed at ethnic Chinese living in other parts of Asia, it wasn't unusual. Such prejudice also existed — perhaps more subtly but existed all the same — in countries like the Philippines and Thailand, where ethnic Chinese controlled large parts of the economy. In those countries, in particular, it was still common for ethnic Chinese to adopt local names.

He read the information Ava had given him on Bank

Linno. If such a bank existed, Chung would know about it. Uncle checked the time. Jakarta was an hour behind Hong Kong, and if Chung was anything like him, he would have been up for several hours already.

Uncle left the park and made his way to his apartment. Lourdes had left a note saying she had gone shopping. He guessed she was actually socializing with some of the local Filipina nannies and housekeepers. Either way, Uncle was pleased to have the apartment to himself. He located his contact book and found Chung's number. The phone rang five times before he heard a faint voice say something in Indonesian.

"Chung, this is Uncle from Hong Kong."

"What a surprise," Chung said. "I know you won't believe this, but I was just talking about you with some of my friends last week."

"Not unkindly, I hope."

"Never. We were just curious what you were up to."

"I started a debt collection business after I stepped down from my official duties with the brotherhood. I'm still at it. In fact, that's why I'm calling. I could use your help on a job."

"What is it I can do for you, Uncle?" asked Chung.

"Have you heard of a Bank Linno?"

"No."

"I'm told it is headquartered in Surabaya."

"That is entirely possible. We have many local banks in this country."

"Could you look into it for me?" asked Uncle.

"Of course. What do you want to know?"

"How large is it? What kind of business does it do? Who owns it? And anything else you might uncover."

"I'll make some calls. How do I reach you?"

"I'm calling from my home line. Does the number show?"

"Yes."

"If I don't answer, then you can phone my mobile," Uncle said and recited his number.

"I'll get right on it," said Chung.

"One more thing," said Uncle. "My partner may need to visit Surabaya. If she needs any help, can you arrange it?"

"I don't have any men there, but it is only an hour's flight from here, so I can get someone there in a hurry if you need them."

"That is good to know, and of course I would pay for the men and their expenses," Uncle said — an offer he hadn't made to Phan, a fellow triad. But Chung was a jago, and the sense of obligation wasn't as keen.

"I wouldn't hear of it," Chung said sharply.

"Thank you, Chung," Uncle said, pleased that he still valued their past ties.

"You are welcome. I'll be in touch."

Uncle put down the phone and rested his head against the back of the chair. The lethargy he'd felt when he woke seemed to have taken over every muscle in his body. He closed his eyes, took several deep breaths, and tried to think of something more pleasant. Replaying horse races in his mind always calmed him, and he thought of the third race from the night before. He watched the horses as they entered the starting gate, and noted with satisfaction that his choice, number four, did so routinely. It was a twelve-horse field running a distance of 1,650 metres, so a good start, while always beneficial, wasn't necessary. Still, he felt confident when he saw his horse break well. The jockey positioned him in third, only a couple of lengths behind the leader...

9

UNCLE HEARD A PHONE RINGING IN THE DISTANCE AND wondered whose it was. He tried to open his eyes but they felt glued shut. He realized he'd been sleeping, and started to turn sideways as if to get out of bed, only to be blocked by the arms of a chair.

"He's been sleeping for hours," he heard Lourdes say. Then there was long pause, and she said, "No, I couldn't do that. But when he wakes, I'll tell him you called."

He sat upright. "Lourdes, what's going on?"

Flustered, she hung up the phone. "That was Sonny. It was the third time he's called. He just wanted you to know that Ava got off on time, and then he was wondering if you needed him for anything."

Uncle was facing the window and noticed that the streetlights were on. He looked at his watch and saw it was almost eight o'clock. It hadn't been much later than mid-morning when he called Chung. Disconcertingly, he realized he had slept away the entire day. He rose to his feet and went directly to the bathroom. He slapped cold water on his face and returned to the living room, where Lourdes stood uncomfortably by her bedroom door.

"Can I get you anything to eat or drink, sir?"

"Not right now," he said. "Did anyone else call?"

"Yes, Mr. Fong and a man named Chung."

"What did Mr. Fong want?"

"He didn't say."

"And Mr. Chung?"

"He said to tell you that he has the information you asked for."

"Good, I'll phone him first," Uncle said. He looked at his chair and decided he had to get away from it. He collected his contact book and cell phone and left the apartment.

It was much noisier outside than it had been when he'd made calls from there a few nights before. Uncle walked along the street until he came to the recessed entrance of a closed store. He stepped inside and phoned Jakarta.

"Chung, this is Uncle. Sorry I missed your call earlier."

"Not to worry."

"What have you found out about Bank Linno?"

"Well, it does exist, and its headquarters are in Surabaya. Aside from its operations there, it has a few branches scattered across the rest of East Java province. It has been around for decades, and its client base has mostly been local farmers and fishermen."

"It has no presence anywhere else?"

"We thought it might have a branch in Jakarta, but it seems to be entirely local to East Java."

"Then what is it doing with a branch in Toronto, Canada?"

"Is that a joke?" Chung asked.

"No, I was told the bank had a branch in Toronto. It closed recently, but it was there and doing business."

"That's odd. There are a few other puzzling details that we uncovered," said Chung.

"Such as?"

"For one, we were told its asset base has significantly expanded over the past several years."

"Who told you that?"

"We have a connection at the Ministry of Finance whose brother works for the division that regulates banks."

"What did he think was responsible for the increase?"

"He said the bank's ownership changed about six years ago, and suggested the new owners were behind the infusion," said Chung.

"That sounds reasonable."

"Except there were some things related to the ownership change that struck our connection as strange," Chung said. "Specifically, the laws here dictate that all banks must be owned by Indonesians. Officially, and on the record, the new owners appear to be Indonesian, but the president is British. Our contact thought that was unusual enough to mention. I mean, why is a British banker running a small local bank in East Java?"

"Have the bank regulators in Jakarta looked into it?"

"They have no reason to. The bank appears to be following all the rules and regulations, and there is no law against hiring foreigners."

"Well, there's no point in us speculating about it. I'll pass this information along to my partner. If there is something more to this bank than appears on the surface, she will be able to unearth it," Uncle said. "I still don't know if she'll be going to Surabaya, but if she does, I'll be in touch again."

"I'm here for you. Call me anytime," said Chung.

Uncle thought briefly about calling Ava but didn't want to disturb her. When they were on a job, their pattern was always for Ava to reach out to him when the need arose, and rarely the reverse, unless there was something of real importance to share. As interesting as it was, he didn't think the Bank Linno information had any urgency attached to it. So, instead, he phoned Fong.

"Ah, Uncle, my least favourite customer," Fong answered.

"I had a good night," Uncle laughed. "But I'm not always that lucky, and hopefully I won't have to use the services of the betting shop again."

"Do you want me to close the account? I can bring you the cash."

"No, leave it there for now," Uncle said, thinking that the treatments scheduled in the coming weeks might keep him at home again.

Before Fong could reply, Uncle's phone beeped, and he saw Ava's cell number. "I have an incoming call from Ava that I have to take. I'll touch base with you tomorrow," he said quickly, then switched lines. "How are things in Ho Chi Minh City?" he answered. "Did you get the help you needed?"

"I did, thanks."

"And have you managed to corner Lam yet?"

"Yes, and it wasn't very difficult — he was waiting for someone to show up, for someone to confess to."

"Some people cannot carry guilt."

"It was more fear than guilt," she said.

"It is hard to tell the difference sometimes. So, what is his story?"

"It's more complicated than we thought," she said.

"The money is gone?"

"I don't know for certain, but the people who Lam says stole it are dead."

"Dead?"

"Yes — decapitated actually. I'm looking at pictures of their heads sitting on a chair as we speak."

Uncle felt a chill run down his spine. "This is not what we expected."

"It's a bizarre story."

"I am listening," he said.

"Well, Lam told me he put the money into something called the Surabaya Fidelity Fund, which he thought was legitimate. A close friend, a man named Purslow who worked at Bank Linno, told him about the fund. He said it was reserved for special customers of the bank, and that its returns were guaranteed. Lam bought the story and started depositing the money from his clients into it. The fund paid a dividend to Lam every month. He deducted two percent, which he split with Purslow, and passed the balance along to his clients."

"Was that enough to keep them happy?"

"Oh yes, and they kept putting more money into the fund until —"

"Their dividends stopped."

"Exactly. And when they did, Lam went to Purslow, who told him there was a glitch in the bank's accounting system and that it would take a few days to sort out," said Ava. "When those days had passed, Lam tried to contact Purslow again but got a voice message that said he was on holiday. Lam panicked and went to the bank. After some considerable confusion, he finally met with two senior bank officers.

They informed him that the Emerald Lion Fund did not have an account at the bank, and that it appeared the money had gone into a numbered account that was controlled by Purslow. Furious, Lam threatened to go to the police. The bank officers convinced him to hold off for a week until they could find out more about what had happened to the money. As an inducement, they offered to pay the dividend that had been missed. Lam agreed."

"When did he hear from them again?"

"The next day, one of the officers called him to say that the money had been transferred offshore, but he wouldn't tell him where. Instead, Lam was told the bank would take matters into its own hands and he wasn't to worry. They said they would find Purslow and return the money to Lam. Until they did, they wanted Lam to stay quiet, and offered to keep paying the monthly dividends until the matter was fully resolved."

"What were the officers' names?"

"Muljadi and Rocca."

"Muljadi is Indonesian, and Rocca sounds Italian, though he could be from anywhere," said Uncle. "Did either of them ever reach out to Lam again?"

"Not directly. When the week was up, he tried calling them without success, and then went back to the bank. He found it shuttered. Next, he contacted the landlords to see if they had any information. They had none they were willing to share. When he told them he was going to go to the police, they said that wasn't a good idea," she said. "The following day, as he was leaving his apartment, Lam was accosted by two bikers who told him to back off or risk getting hurt. He debated about what to do until a few days later, when a brown envelope was shoved under his door. It contained a newspaper article from the *Tico Times* in Costa Rica, with a photo of two men's heads on a chair. The article was about the murder of two Canadian tourists. One of them was Purslow."

"Lam must have been terrified."

"Enough that the next day he caught a plane to Ho Chi Minh City," she said.

"So what does Lam believe now, after he's had some time to think about it? Did the bank have Purslow killed?"

"He thinks it's very possible, and on the whole I don't disagree with him."

"You believe his story?"

"I do. I felt he was telling me as much of the truth as he knew," she said. "And before I left, he gave me all of his financial records relating to the fund, including his initial agreement, deposits, and the payouts."

Ava's recounting of Lam's story was so gripping that Uncle found it difficult to stay still as he listened. He left the store entranceway and started walking along the street. When she finished, he realized he'd gone about a kilometre without being aware of it.

"From everything you've told me, it seems the money is most likely out of reach," he said.

There was a short silence from Ava, and then she said, "I still want to try to find it."

Uncle turned and began to retrace his steps. "Ava, if you set your mind to it, I know you might be able to find the money. What I am saying is that it may not be worth the risk. We do not know who is at the other end of the money trail. All we know is that they were prepared to kill two men to keep its whereabouts a secret."

"I'm not ready to give up," she said. "We still have a link to Lam and the money: Bank Linno. Let's find out what we can about it. I'm going to call Johnny Yan at the Toronto Commonwealth Bank to ask if he knows anything about the bank, Muljadi, and Rocca."

"I already have some information," Uncle said, and then repeated what Chung had told him earlier.

Ava hesitated after he finished. "Do you think you could ask him for more detail?"

"What is it you have in mind?" he replied, slightly taken aback by the subtle implication that he had missed something.

"It could be useful to know the name of the British president. If possible, I'd also like to know the level of actual capitalization, and get more information about the owner and how the deal was done."

Uncle found a wall to lean against. He felt his face flush with embarrassment. These were questions he should have asked when he was talking to Chung. Was his mind going to start betraying him now, in addition to his body?

"I'll call my contact as soon as we're finished. I'll tell him we need the information urgently."

10

AN HOUR LATER, UNCLE SAT IN HIS CHAIR WHILE HE waited for Chung to call him back with the information Ava had requested. Chung hadn't been surprised by the questions, and that made Uncle even more sure that he should have thought to ask them during their first conversation.

Lourdes had steamed rice for him when he returned from the street, and he had managed to eat two bowls of it. The rice felt like a heavy lump in his stomach, but there was no pain and no nausea. He had washed it down with a glass of water, after resisting the temptation to take a bottle of San Miguel from the fridge. *If I still feel okay in a couple of days*, he thought, *maybe I'll take a sip or two of beer and try to expand my diet.*

As he contemplated moving beyond plain white rice and congee, his phone rang and Uncle saw the Indonesian country code.

"Chung, thank you for getting back to me so quickly," he answered.

"This is Perkasa. I'm Chung's son. My father had to go to a meeting and asked me to call you when we had the information you requested."

"You know the contact?"

"I went to university with him."

"Ah," Uncle said, realizing that time was passing Chung by as well as him. "I very much appreciate the help you are providing."

"You are a man who has earned that help. My father and his colleagues think the world of you, and I am someone who respects those who have gone before me."

"That is kind of you to say."

"It is simply the truth," said Perkasa. "Now, can I relay what I've learned?"

"Please."

"The president of the bank is named Andy Cameron. He is British, but of Scottish descent, and my understanding from my university days in Singapore is that the Scots don't like being referred to as British."

"How unusual is it for an Indonesian bank to have a president who isn't Indonesian?"

"This is the only occurrence my contact knows."

"What about capitalization?"

"It has grown by hundreds of millions every year since Cameron arrived. In fact, my contact estimates it is now about twenty times higher than it was before the change in leadership."

"Are those U.S. dollars?"

"They are, and the bank's capitalization is now around four billion of them," said Perkasa. "For a bank that doesn't rank in the top fifty in the country in terms of the number of branches and employees, that is a remarkable sum."

"Your father said the bank was sold just before Cameron became president."

"It was. It was founded about fifty years ago, and until recently it operated only in East Java. A small-time operation. Cameron's hiring and the influx of capital started as soon as the new owners took over," Perkasa said.

"The connection between Cameron, new ownership, and the influx can't be coincidental," Uncle said.

"Probably not, but as far as my contact knows there is nothing illegal going on."

"If there was, could government officials be persuaded to turn a blind eye?"

Perkasa laughed. "They most certainly could. Making money on the side is a time-honoured tradition in our national government."

"Who are the new owners?"

"A couple of local East Java businessmen are the majority shareholders, but I was told they are likely frontmen for bigger fish."

"Foreigners?"

"Possibly, but not necessarily."

Uncle searched his mind for more questions he could ask about the bank and found none that weren't repetitive, so he switched gears. "I think my partner, Ava Lee, will be travelling to Surabaya tomorrow to look into the bank. Your father told me he would send someone from Jakarta to provide help if she needed it. Do you have any idea who that might be?"

"Yes, it would be me."

"I had assumed since you went to university that you wouldn't be in your father's line of work."

"Well, I am. I'm a jago like him, and I'm proud of it."

"And if my partner needs active support?"

"I can't think of anything she could request that I couldn't deliver."

"She is a very capable young woman, but she'll be working in an unknown environment," Uncle said. "Hopefully she won't need your assistance, but it is comforting to know you are on standby."

"You can count on me," said Perkasa.

"Thank you, and pass along my thanks to your father as well," Uncle said.

He felt a sense of relief as he hung up, then he quickly hit Ava's mobile number. He was certain that Perkasa would be a tremendous asset.

"I have the information you wanted," Uncle said as soon as he heard her voice.

"That's wonderful, and I found out some things too," she said. "You go first."

Uncle related what Perkasa had told him, and then explained who Perkasa was and how useful he might be.

"Having someone on the ground you can trust is so valuable, and as it turns out I may have someone else to lend a hand," Ava said. "I spoke to Johnny Yan, who gave me the name of a Canadian friend, John Masterson, who operates a business in Surabaya. My hope is that the friend knows this Andy Cameron. If he does, I'll use him to make an introduction."

"How likely is that?" Uncle asked.

"There can't be that many ex-pats in Surabaya, and my experience is that those who are living in a place like that tend to know each other."

"I hope you're right."

"If not, I'll find another way to connect with Cameron.

There is definitely something odd going on with this bank, and he seems to be at the centre of it."

"Explain what you mean by 'odd'?"

"Well, according to Johnny, it wasn't actually registered as a bank in Canada. It was what he called a 'near-bank,' which provided limited services to a select group of customers. If Lam had done any serious digging into it, he would have found that out and maybe avoided doing business with them."

"What kind of services did it provide?"

"Bank Linno put most of its money into real estate. That isn't strange on the surface, but it was predominantly in parts of the city that have large Italian populations," Ava said. "Why would an Indonesian bank implement that as a strategy?"

"Maybe the man Rocca had something to do with it?"

"That's my thought as well," she said. "And by the way, his first name is Dominic. He's known to Johnny, but he seems to have disappeared, as has Muljadi. I can understand why Muljadi might have left when the branch closed, but Rocca was a local and had a lot of banking connections. Why wouldn't he simply look for work with another bank?"

"Perhaps Bank Linno transferred him?"

"But where? According to Johnny, the only other branch they had in North America was in New York City, and it appears to have closed months before the one in Toronto."

"It does sound odd, and that's all the more reason for you to be careful," Uncle said.

"Don't worry, I'm not going to do anything risky," she said.

"When do you leave Ho Chi Minh?"

"I have a flight booked for early tomorrow morning to Hong Kong, where I can connect with a direct flight to Surabaya."

"Is it a tight connection?"

"No, but I'm not sure it will give me enough time to come into the city," she said. "If you come to the airport, maybe we could meet for dim sum?"

Uncle paused as he gauged what was on a dim sum menu that wouldn't unsettle his stomach. "That sounds like it could work. You'll have to update me in the morning."

"I'll call you before we depart."

"Seeing you twice in two days is a treat."

Uncle waited a few minutes before calling Sonny. He didn't like the way Sonny was quizzing Lourdes about him, but on the other hand, if he made a fuss it might make Sonny even more suspicious. He knew Sonny was simply concerned and didn't deserve to be rebuked. But Uncle also didn't want to leave the door open for questions, however well-intentioned they might be. He decided to keep their conversation short.

"Boss, good to hear from you," Sonny answered.

"I'll need you tomorrow morning," Uncle said. "Ava is arriving from Ho Chi Minh City and we're going to meet at the airport. I'll call you as soon as I know the time."

"I'll be ready."

"Great, but I don't have time to talk right now," Uncle said quickly. "We'll touch base again tomorrow."

(11)

UNCLE SLEPT BETTER, BUT STILL WOKE IN TIME TO SEE
the sun creep over the horizon. Twenty minutes later he left
the apartment and made his way to the newsstand to buy
his papers and the racing form for Sunday's card at Sha Tin.

Suki greeted him at Morning Blessings, led him to his
table, and after taking his order for plain congee with a glass
of water, asked, "Uncle, are you feeling all right?"

"My doctor wants me to go easy with my food choices
for a few days. My cholesterol is higher than it should be."

"My husband has the same problem," she said.

"We're at that age —"

"Neither of you look your age," she said quickly.

"Perhaps not, but our bodies don't care about how we
look on the outside."

Suki smiled. "Listen to your doctor."

"I am."

For the next hour he worked his way through the newspapers and the congee that soon became cold. Suki twice
offered to bring him a fresh bowl, but he told her not to
bother. Cold or hot, the congee tasted the same to him. He

was about to turn his attention to the racing form when his phone rang, and he saw Ava's number.

"*Wei*, Ava," he said.

"I'm at the airport in Ho Chi Minh, and I managed to change my flight to tighten the connection in Hong Kong," she said. "I hope you don't mind, but we should probably skip dim sum. I think getting to Surabaya as soon as I can should be the priority."

"Of course," Uncle said.

"I'm going to reach out to Johnny's friend to see if he knows Cameron. If he does, that's the easiest route to a meeting. I'll need a cover story, and I'm hoping you can talk to Dynamic Financial Services about that."

"What do you need?"

"I thought I would tell Cameron that I'm in Surabaya working for Dynamic on behalf of some clients who are looking for a local bank."

"Why do the clients need a local bank?"

"They're thinking of investing in vacation properties. That makes sense given the growth in tourism in the area."

"Then that's what Dynamic will tell anyone who calls to confirm why you are in Surabaya. What name will you be using?"

"My own. I already have a Dynamic business card with my name on it."

"I'll look after it."

"Thanks — and Uncle, I'm sorry about the last-minute change of plans."

"There's nothing to be sorry about," he said. "Call me when you land in Surabaya and you know what your schedule is like."

He checked the time, saw it was too early to call Dynamic, but knew Sonny would be waiting. He wasn't going to like being inactive for another day. Uncle needed to find something that would keep him occupied and out of his hair. An idea came to mind, and he phoned Fong.

"Yes," Fong answered in a voice full of sleep.

"Did I wake you?"

"You know you did. When do I ever get out of bed so early?"

"I'm sorry, but I need a favour."

"What is it?"

"I haven't been using Sonny this week. He's antsy, and frankly getting on my nerves. I need something for him to do," said Uncle.

"What do you have in mind?"

"Do you have any upcoming business trips planned? I was hoping that you might be going to Shenzhen or someplace like that."

"I was supposed to go to Guangzhou this week, but I've been putting it off."

"Why don't you go there today and use Sonny as your driver?"

Fong didn't immediately respond, but then said, "You do know that this sounds a bit strange. Why haven't you been using him?"

"I've had this stomach issue all week and I haven't felt comfortable leaving the apartment. I don't want to say anything to Sonny because he'll start harassing Lourdes about my health and likely drag Ava into it. This way I can keep him busy for the day."

"If you say so," said Fong, not sounding entirely convinced.

"How is your health? Do I need to worry?"

"No. Like I told you before, I've had an upset stomach, that's all. I'm taking something for it, but it takes time. Just do this for me, will you?"

"Of course, Uncle. Tell Sonny he can pick me up in an hour."

"Thanks, Fong. Keep him as long as you need."

Uncle disliked the idea of lying to Fong, and preferred to think that he was simply withholding the truth. Until he was certain about his situation, that's what he was going to continue to do, he thought as he called Sonny.

"*Wei,*" Sonny answered.

"Ava has changed her plans. You won't be meeting her at the airport, but I have something else I'd like you to do for me today," Uncle said.

"What's that, boss?"

"Fong has to go to Guangzhou on business and wondered if you could drive him. I told him it was fine with me, but I wanted to check with you."

"If you don't need me —"

"I'll manage, and I do owe Fong a few favours."

"When do you want me to go?"

"Fong is expecting you at his place in an hour."

With Sonny settled, Uncle turned his attention back to the racing form. After a quick scan, he decided to continue his reading back at the apartment. It was warmer outside than it had been for several weeks, and he thought about taking a taxi before deciding to walk. He went slowly, conscious of not overexerting himself, but even then, by the time he had gone half the distance, a numbing weariness overcame him. He stopped at the park and found a bench to sit on.

The recent issues with his stomach aside, Uncle had never experienced any serious illness. There had been times when his body had been damaged, but those were injuries imposed by third parties, and they had gradually healed. This was different. There was no healing on the horizon. The best he could hope for was to slow the cancer's advance.

Uncle had, he realized, still not fully grasped the impact the treatments might have on him. Now, he found himself questioning how much quality of life he was prepared to sacrifice to buy more time. He lit a cigarette and looked up into the sun. How could the outside world appear so normal when he was in such turmoil?

Uncle made a mental note to speak to May Ling when he felt more on top of things. Like him, she followed the Way of the Tao — the way of the natural order of the universe — enjoying life day-to-day without any fear of death. And if death came, they would experience *shijie* — a release from their corpse — and either be transformed or ascend to heaven. Uncle wasn't convinced about transformation or heaven, but he was prepared to believe there was an afterlife, even if it was in a form he hadn't anticipated. He was curious to know what May thought.

He wasn't aware of how much time passed as he sat on the bench, until he looked at his watch and saw he had been there for a couple of hours. He immediately reached for his phone to call Margaret Chew, the owner of Dynamic Financial Services.

In Fanling, the gang did its own accounting, and Uncle had never had the need of an outside firm. His move to Kowloon changed his circumstances, and he had, on the recommendation of the president of the Kowloon Light and

Power Bank, hired Dynamic. In addition to handling his accounts and taxes, Margaret Chew had been amenable to providing cover for Ava on several jobs. Uncle had offered her a small fee for the service, but she had refused.

A receptionist answered his call and put him through to Margaret.

"It has been quite some time since we spoke," she said.

"Ava and I were taking a small break from the business, but we're back on the job and need your help," he said.

"What is it this time?" Margaret asked, sounding amused.

"Ava is in Surabaya, Indonesia. Her story is that she works for Dynamic and is there to investigate real estate investment opportunities for a Hong Kong–based client," he said. "She is also looking for a local bank the client can use. You might get some calls to verify her story."

"I will tell our receptionist to put any calls concerning Ava through to me," said Margaret. "Do you want me to advise you if someone does enquire about her?"

"Yes, that information might be useful," Uncle said. "Thank you once again, Margaret."

He rose from the bench and started to walk in the direction of his apartment. He knew he was going to pass a bakery on the way and considered going in. If congee and white rice didn't negatively affect his body, then why not try a bun? And if the bun was covered in coconut, then so much the better.

BETWEEN READING THE RACING FORM, TAKING A NAP, and a stomach that handled the coconut bun well, Uncle's afternoon was peaceful and relaxed. He checked the time frequently, calculating when Ava would be landing in Surabaya and be reachable by phone. He tried to call at four, but his call went directly to voicemail. He was about to try again at five when his phone rang, and he saw her number.

"You have arrived safely?" he asked.

"Yes, and I've just spoken to John Masterson, the Canadian who lives here," Ava said. "He knows Cameron and has agreed to introduce us. Masterson is going to invite Cameron to join us for dinner. He says that Cameron is single and often at loose ends on a Friday night, so I'm hopeful he'll accept. If not, I might have to wait until the bank is open for business on Monday."

"Well, whenever you meet with him you can use your Dynamic cover story. Margaret will back you up."

"Excellent."

"Keep me updated, please. I'm always nervous when we're operating in places we don't fully understand," he said.

All things considered, Uncle thought they were off to a decent start in Surabaya. Dynamic was onside, Perkasa was on standby, and he was especially pleased that Ava would be introduced to Cameron rather than having to approach him cold.

He walked to the window. The street was busy, and that discouraged any idea he had of going for a walk, but he wanted to get out of the apartment. He thought about the Nepalese restaurant downstairs. There were some items that he imagined he could eat, as long as they weren't heavily spiced.

Uncle put on a jacket and knocked on Lourdes's door. "I'm going out for dinner. I'm not sure when I'll be back. If Fong or Ava calls, tell them to try my mobile," he said.

He left the apartment, and a moment later was warmly greeted by Anjay.

"Are you here for beer to take away?" Anjay asked.

"I came for dinner, but my stomach is a bit sensitive, and I can't handle anything that's too spicy. What do you have that won't upset it?"

"How about food that's sweet?"

"I ate a coconut bun earlier and it was fine."

"Then we'll be able to look after you," said Ajay. "Let's find a table where you can spread out your racing form."

Over the next few hours, Uncle ate his way slowly and carefully through a plate of momo, dumplings stuffed with vegetables, with mayonnaise on the side; yomari, rice dough stuffed with a sweet paste made of coconut and molasses; and juju dhau, a sweet creamy yogurt made from buffalo milk. The serving sizes were modest, but he still couldn't finish the dishes. He drank water as he ate and fought off the temptation to order a beer until the very end of the meal. He took a sip of the San Miguel and waited to see how his body reacted. When nothing unusual happened, he sipped again, and kept sipping until the bottle was empty.

He felt stuffed and a bit light-headed as he climbed the stairs to his apartment.

"There were no calls, sir," Lourdes said before he could ask.

He nodded, looked at his chair, and decided he'd spent enough time in it that day. "I'm going to lie down. Don't disturb me unless Ava phones."

Uncle closed his eyes when he lay down, more to give his eyes a rest than anything else. Sometime later he woke in darkness. He climbed out of bed and went to the bathroom. He checked his watch and to his shock saw it was almost six a.m. *I missed Ava's call*, he thought, *but why didn't Lourdes wake me?*

His first reaction was to knock on Lourdes's door, and then he realized it would probably frighten her. Instead, he checked his mobile. There were no messages and there had been no calls. He picked up the landline and got the same result. What was going on? This wasn't like her. Even if she hadn't been able to meet with Cameron, or had met with him and it was a bust, he couldn't imagine her not updating him.

Uncle went to the kitchen. He started to pour a glass of water, and then thought, *To hell with it*, and made a black coffee. His stomach burned when the coffee first hit it, but then eased enough that he kept drinking. He debated phoning Sonny to see if he had heard from Ava, but why would she call Sonny and not him? He looked at his watch again. Maybe her dinner had finished late and she had decided to hold off calling him until the morning? He realized it was early to phone her, but he also knew he would have no peace of mind until they spoke. He reached for his mobile and hit her number. Her phone was off and he was sent directly to voicemail.

"Ava, this is Uncle. It is around six o'clock here on Saturday morning. I expected you to call last night, and I'm worried that you didn't. Let me know what's happened. My mobile will be on and by my side," he said.

He thought about showering but didn't want to leave the phone for even a few minutes. So he simply shaved, washed, and changed his clothes. He drank a second coffee without incident, and with still no word from Ava, left the apartment for the walk to the newsstand and Morning Blessings.

Time at the restaurant passed slowly, and he was almost too distracted to read the newspapers. He called Ava's phone twice more and both calls went straight to voicemail. He simply said, "It is Uncle. Call me."

He stopped at the park on the way home and sat on a bench with the phone in his hand, willing it to ring. When after an hour it hadn't, he called the apartment.

"This is Uncle. I'm at the park. Has Ava phoned?"

"No, sir," said Lourdes.

"Did she call last night?"

"No."

"If she does call, tell her to try me on my mobile."

"Yes, sir."

He tried to remember if Ava had said what hotel she was staying at, but if she had, he couldn't recall it. He knew logically there was a strong possibility he was being irrational, but his emotions were overpowering his logic. *Something has happened to her*, he thought suddenly and with certainty. As he did, he felt his face flush, his stomach knot, and his legs go weak. He tried to stand, but his legs caved and he collapsed onto the ground.

A young man and woman rushed to his side and looked down at him in alarm.

"I've just had a shock. If you help me to my feet, I should be okay," Uncle said.

"You don't look well. You need to see a doctor," the woman said. "We can call for an ambulance."

"That's not necessary, I'll be fine, but I would appreciate it if you could get me a taxi."

The couple raised him gently to his feet. He took several deep breaths and began to feel his strength return.

"We'll walk with you to the park entrance. There's a cab stand there," the woman said.

Fifteen minutes later, Uncle exited a taxi in front of his building. He contemplated the three flights of stairs and decided he'd make it if he took his time. He did, but only after five minutes and three stops. He slumped into his chair while Lourdes hovered nearby.

"I'll have a glass of water, please," he said.

He finished one glass and asked for another. As he drank, he could feel his equilibrium steadying. *The episode at the park*, he thought, *was a physical reaction to emotions that were out of my control.* Now, calmer, he realized there was a way he might find out what was going on in Surabaya. He phoned Indonesia.

When Perkasa answered, Uncle could hear a lot of noise in the background.

"This is Uncle," he said loudly.

"I know. I can see your number," Perkasa said. "I'm waiting for a cab to take me to the airport. I'm heading to Surabaya today."

"Are you going at Ava's request?"

"There would be no other reason."

"When did you last speak to her?"

"About an hour ago."

"Did she say why she needed you?"

"Not specifically," Perkasa said, and then paused. "But I don't think it is for anything trivial, because she asked me if I knew men there that I could employ. I said I knew two whom I trusted, and she said she thought that might be enough."

"Enough for what?"

"I'm not sure, but I think there's a chance it could be something unusual."

"Why do you say that?"

Perkasa hesitated, before saying, "I don't know what to make of it, but she asked me if I could buy a picana."

"What's a picana?" Uncle asked.

"An electric cattle prod."

"That does sound unusual," said Uncle, trying to remain calm. "But listen, Perkasa, please do whatever she asks. I know your father didn't want to discuss money with me, but hiring men shouldn't be at your expense. I'm going to send fifty thousand HK dollars to his bank account, and if you need more, I'll send that too. Nothing is more important to me than making sure Ava is safe."

"I'll do whatever is necessary to make sure she is."

Uncle felt an odd mixture of relief and worry. Ava had spoken to Perkasa, which meant she was okay, but why hadn't she called him? And what was she up to in Surabaya that required hired men and a cattle prod?

Uncle rested his head against the back of the chair as he thought about what to do next. Before he made any decisions, his phone rang and he saw Ava's number. He waited until the third ring before answering.

"Uncle, it's Ava."

"How's it going?" he asked, as low-key as he could. "I had expected to hear from you last night."

"Sorry, the dinner ran late, and I slept in this morning," she said in a rush. "Andy Cameron, the CEO of Bank Linno, was with us. He's a sneaky little guy. I tried to get him to open up about the bank and its operations, but he was completely evasive. There's something strange going on there. I can feel it."

Uncle noticed an odd tone in Ava's voice. *Something has happened*, he thought, *but this isn't the time to press the issue*.

"This strange thing you mention — will it have any relevance to our clients?"

"I don't know. But here's something else. I had assumed Cameron was recruited in Asia. As it turns out, he was working for a bank in Rome when he was hired to work for Bank Linno."

The mention of Rome instantly conjured up possible connections that Uncle wasn't ready to pursue. "What else did you get out of him?"

"Almost nothing. I asked about Linno's international business, and he slammed the door on me."

"So what do you want to do?"

"I've asked Perkasa to come to Surabaya," she said, and then paused.

"Yes, he told me," Uncle said, wondering how Ava would react.

She didn't miss a beat. "I think it's time we had a private conversation with Cameron, one in which he'll be more amenable to answering questions. If it leads to nothing, then I'll be back in Hong Kong in a day or two."

"What if he doesn't agree to that kind of conversation?"

"I don't plan on giving him a choice."

"Ava, do you think this is worth that kind of trouble?"

"We have clients; we owe them our best. I don't know any other way to get to the truth about what happened between Lam, Purslow, and the bank."

"Perkasa arrives today?"

"This afternoon," she said.

"When will you confront Cameron?"

"I'll be aiming for early tomorrow morning."

"Well, if it has to be done, it has to be done," Uncle said. "Just make sure there are no repercussions if it turns out badly. I don't want you getting into trouble over there."

"I'll be careful."

"And stay in touch."

"As always," she said.

And not like last night, he wanted to say, but didn't. *Ava sounds troubled*, he thought, *and if she is, the last thing she needs is me scolding her.*

(13)

UNCLE SAT QUIETLY IN HIS CHAIR REPLAYING HIS CON-versations with Perkasa and Ava. If her plan was to abduct Cameron, then he could only assume that the cattle prod would have a role to play. The thought alarmed him, partially because of the prod and what she might do with it, but more because of his confusion about what could have motivated her to request it. On humans, the prod's only use was as an instrument of torture, and torture had never been how they operated. If that was Ava's intent, then he was certain something had happened to push her to that decision. But what was it, and should he ask or let it pass?

Uncle and Ava had always had what he considered their own little secrets. For example, he had never discussed Gui-San with her, although he was sure Fong had. Similarly, she had never spoken about her sexual orientation even though he had met women she dated, and she must have assumed he knew. Part of that reticence, he thought, was an indication of how much they respected each other's privacy. So if Ava didn't want to explain why she wanted the cattle prod, it wasn't for him to insist. Just as he was entitled to keep his illness secret from her and everyone else.

Still, even if he respected Ava's privacy, that didn't prevent him from worrying. He briefly considered calling Perkasa again to emphasize his concerns, but realized he had nothing new to say. He sighed. The prospect of a day and night with nothing to do while he waited to hear how events unfolded in Surabaya was unappealing. He needed to do something, and as he worked through his options, one came to mind for which the time had probably come. He reached for the phone and called Fong.

"Hey, Uncle," Fong answered.

"I was wondering how your day in Guangzhou went?"

"Routine business, nothing more, and it all went well."

"And what about Sonny? Was he okay?"

"He was a bit more talkative than usual," said Fong. "And truthfully, he was asking me questions about you. He's worried about your health."

"That's one reason I wanted to get him out of my hair."

"Is there anything to worry about, Uncle?"

"No," Uncle said abruptly. "Are you in Fanling?"

"Yes."

"Do you have plans to go to Macau?"

"We're expecting a busy Sunday afternoon with the Sha Tin races so I won't be going over until they're finished."

"And what is your schedule like today?"

"It's open."

"Good, there is something I would like you to do with me."

"What's that?"

"I'll tell you when I see you," Uncle said. "How is it for you if I get there in an hour or so?"

"No problem."

"See you then," said Uncle.

Sonny answered on the first ring. "Yes, boss."

"Is your day and evening clear?"

"If they weren't, they are now."

"Am I taking you away from your girlfriend?"

"She knows it comes with the territory."

"Then could you pick me up in the next half hour and take me to Fanling? I'm meeting Fong, and from there we'll be going to Yuen Long, and maybe dinner later at Dong's," he said, not surprised by Sonny's answer.

Ever since he'd started driving for Uncle, Sonny's devotion had taken precedence over everything, including his personal life. Sonny had never married, but there had been girlfriends, some of whom Uncle had met. The current one had been around for several years, and Uncle wondered how she reacted when her Saturdays were disrupted like this one was going to be. *Well*, he thought, *it isn't my problem.*

Uncle went into the bathroom to freshen up and then knocked on Lourdes's door. "I'll be gone for the day. If there are any calls, direct them to my mobile," he said.

Once outside, Uncle lit a cigarette, took a couple of puffs, and then threw it away. Despite Doctor Parker's indifference to him smoking, his taste for it had waned. Maybe it was another reaction to the chemo, he thought, or perhaps a subconscious rejection of the thing that had caused his cancer.

Uncle stood watching pedestrians go by, and was struck by how disconnected he felt from them. They seemed unreal and beyond his understanding. A honking car horn took his attention away from the sidewalk, and he saw Sonny parked directly in front of him.

As was his habit, Sonny started to get out of the car to open the back door, but Uncle waved him off and climbed in.

"I'm sorry I honked, but I was sitting here for a minute, and you didn't seem to see me," said Sonny.

"I was daydreaming," said Uncle.

Sonny nodded as if that was something natural for Uncle to be doing. "So, our first stop is Fanling?"

"Yes, Fong's apartment," Uncle said, taking out the racing form that he'd stuffed into his jacket pocket. It was a signal to Sonny that he didn't want to indulge in conversation.

Traffic was light, and the twenty-kilometre trip took less than half an hour. Uncle called Fong from the car when they arrived, and a moment later Fong joined them.

"Now, let's head for Yuen Long," Uncle said to Sonny as Fong settled in the back seat beside him.

"What's in Yuen Long?" Fong asked.

"The Ancestor Worship Hall on Fo Look Hill," said Uncle.

Fong pursed his lips, and Uncle saw Sonny stare at him in the rear-view mirror.

"Relax, both of you. I'm not going there to buy a niche. I already have a plot reserved for me at the Fanling cemetery, and I'm in no rush to fill it," Uncle said. He turned to Fong. "I'll explain things to you when we get to the hall."

It was another twenty-kilometre ride, and it passed quickly and quietly. When they neared the hall, traffic slowed, and Uncle knew it was going to be crowded. When he visited, he always went early in the morning, and never on a weekend unless it was Gui-San's birthday, Chinese New Year, or the Qingming Festival.

"Just stop close enough to let us out, and park wherever you can. I'll call you when we're ready to leave," Uncle said to Sonny. "We shouldn't be longer than twenty minutes."

When the car came to a stop, Uncle and Fong climbed out. They stared up a hundred-metre hill to the hall. The path that ran up to it was filled with people coming and going. They joined the line that was going up, and in single file made their way to the top. When they reached it, Uncle veered to the left and went to a wall filled with small alcoves and niches. He stopped and pointed up at an inscription that read:

LIN GUI-SAN

BORN IN CHANGZHAI, HUBEI PROVINCE, 28 OCTOBER 1934

DIED NEAR HONG KONG, 28 JUNE 1959

FOREVER LOVED

FOREVER MISSED

"I've wanted to bring you here for years, but something always seemed to come up," Uncle said.

"I didn't know you found her body," said Fong.

"I didn't. I put sand from the beach in Yuen Long in that urn, and a jade bracelet I was going to give her on the day we were married."

"When did you do that?"

"Not long after she died. I've been coming here ever since, to talk to her. She's very wise."

Fong took a step forward to look more closely at the photo that was on the back wall of the niche. "She was very beautiful," he said.

"I know, but what I remember most is how determined and brave she was. I'm not sure I would have had the courage to leave China if she hadn't been at my side."

Without turning around, Fong asked, "Why are you showing me this now?"

"Like I said, it was something I always intended to do. There's no particular reason for the timing, although there is for the purpose," Uncle said.

"And what is the purpose?"

"Well, as much as I don't like to think about it, and although I hope it isn't for several more years, there is going to come a day when I die," Uncle said. "When I do, I would like you to come here to remove the urn and Gui-San's photo. I will be buried in a casket, and before it is closed, I would appreciate it if you could put the urn and the photo next to me. I don't want anyone else to know about this."

"Will the people who manage this hall just let me take away an urn and photo?"

"I will advise them of my wishes, and I'll give you a letter authorizing the removal."

"Okay," Fong said, turning to look at Uncle. "But what if I die before you do? That's something I've always thought likely."

"Then I will go to someone else I trust."

Fong looked up at the clear, blue sky. "I think that's enough talk about death. On a day like this we should be doing something more cheerful."

"I haven't been to Dong's in a while. I thought we might have dinner there."

"That's a great idea, but would it bother you if some of our brothers joined us? Word will spread that you are at Dong's, and I know a lot of people will want to say hello."

Uncle hesitated, and then thought, *How many more chances will I have to see my old friends in Fanling?*

"It wouldn't bother me in the least."

14

UNCLE HAD A WONDERFUL EVENING THAT WAS FOL-
lowed by a troubled night. The dinner at Dong's began with
Hui, the Fanling Mountain Master, insisting on hosting
them. Despite Uncle's protests, Hui ordered extra-large
dishes that he knew were Uncle's favourites. As the salt and
pepper fried squid, Fukien rice, beef short ribs, and Dong's
famous chicken feet in secret sauce were brought to the table,
Uncle wondered how they would ever finish all of it. But a
steady stream of triads who came to pay their respects to
Uncle were invited to sit and eat a little, and dish by dish
they worked their way through it.

Uncle ate sparingly and carefully, avoiding anything that
was overly spiced, but enjoying the aromas and each bite all
the same. He nursed one beer for most of the evening, and
only succumbed to a second after Hui would not stop insisting. No one commented on his light eating and drinking,
but he noticed Sonny eyeing him suspiciously several times.

The evening was filled with reminiscing as Hui, Fong, and
the triads who joined them shared favourite stories about
Uncle. He couldn't remember all the events they described

and thought his contributions to some of those he did were exaggerated. But there was such a feeling of brotherhood that Uncle simply took it all in with a smile. His social circle had dramatically shrunk after he moved to Kowloon, but it was only at times like this that he realized how much he missed the comradery.

It was past ten o'clock when Sonny drove him home. Uncle's phone hadn't rung since he had left Kowloon, and it had been so busy at Dong's that he hadn't thought about Ava. He was sure he would have heard from her if there had been any problem with Perkasa's arrival in Surabaya, and he was equally sure they would have created a reasonable plan for getting hold of Cameron. Still, he had some nagging worries, partially brought on by the fact Ava had been inactive for so many months, and by — less practically — a vague feeling of discomfort about what she might find out. There was something distinctly odd about the situation in Surabaya, and although he couldn't put a finger on it, Uncle felt disquieted.

"That was a great night," Sonny said, disrupting Uncle's thoughts as they drove south towards Kowloon. "The men were thrilled to see you."

"And I was pleased to see them. There are times that I miss our old life."

"You should go to Fanling more often," Sonny said, and then looked into the rear-view mirror as if he were trying to provoke a response.

"Once every few years is enough. I wouldn't want to become a nuisance."

"That would never be the case."

"That's enough about Fanling. Let's talk about tomorrow."

"Will you be going to Sha Tin for the races?"

"That is my plan, unless something happens with Ava in Surabaya that needs my attention," Uncle said. "If you don't hear from me in the morning, assume we're going and pick me up at eleven-thirty."

"How are things with Ava?"

"She arrived in Surabaya safely, but beyond that I won't know much until tomorrow."

Uncle began to feel fatigued halfway through the ride, and by the time they reached his apartment he was struggling to keep his eyes open. He went immediately to bed expecting to have a solid sleep. But a few hours later he woke with an upset stomach, and for the rest of the night he was in and out of the bathroom.

At seven, he got out of bed feeling dehydrated. He drank two glasses of water and then sat in his chair with the racing form. He still had more than four hours before Sonny was scheduled to pick him up. If his stomach settled, he decided he would go to Sha Tin, but he wanted to be sure there wouldn't be any embarrassing accidents.

He didn't make any more trips to the bathroom until nine, and then it was to shave and shower. His stomach seemed to be under control, and he thought briefly about eating some plain white rice or going to Morning Blessings for congee before deciding that caution should prevail. Uncle went into his bedroom to dress for the day and was still buttoning his shirt when the phone rang. He rushed to it, certain Ava was calling.

"*Wei*," he answered.

"It's Ava. What a morning we've had."

"Were there problems?"

"None of an immediate kind," she said.

"What does that mean?" he asked, ill at ease.

"Uncle, we managed to grab Cameron without difficulty, and I've been able to persuade him to talk. The thing is, we have stumbled into something which is way larger and far more complicated than I imagined," she said. "This bank, the man Cameron, the Indonesian connections — they are nothing but window dressing to hide an immense money-laundering operation."

"Who is doing the laundering?"

"An Italian mob that Cameron says is the 'Ndrangheta. Have you heard of them?"

Uncle immediately felt a nervous chill. "Unfortunately, I have, but more on them later. Tell me what they are doing."

"According to Cameron — and I have no reason to doubt him — they are flying planeloads of cash into Indonesia. The money is deposited into Bank Linno, and then goes back to various 'Ndrangheta associates in the form of loans to buy real estate in places like New York, Rome, and Toronto. The loans, of course, aren't really loans. They are never repaid and there is no interest charged. The bank keeps two sets of books. One set reflects the reality of what's going on, and the other shows that loan payments are being properly made. That second set is what the bank shows to the Indonesian government, and they've even been paying taxes based on their fictional profits."

"I assume the 'Ndrangheta control the bank."

"They own the bank and control every part of its business. There are two members living in Surabaya, and they monitor its operations. Cameron is limited in what he can do as president. He claims the Italians make every important decision," Ava said.

"Could he confirm what happened to the money from Toronto?"

"He could. Purslow stole it, and when the Italians found out they went ballistic. They tracked him down, killed him, and then transferred the money to Surabaya."

"If it is there, can we get our hands on it?"

"Not through Cameron, or so he maintains. He says he doesn't have the authority to complete any transaction over a million dollars without approval. His main job is to provide the cover — the paper trail for those bogus real estate loans," she said. "Although, truthfully, I'm not sure why they felt that was necessary since Cameron says they're paying a lot of Indonesian government officials not to look too hard into what's going on."

"Those particular Italians are as cautious as they are clever — and they are exceedingly clever."

"How do you know them?"

"I met some of their representatives many years ago when they came to Asia to buy drugs. They explained that their gang was bound together by blood, money, and oaths that they valued above their lives. I never did business with them, but some brothers tried, and it didn't turn out well," he said. "There is a viciousness to them that makes them difficult partners, but that also explains why they have done so well. Killing Purslow and keeping Cameron on a tight rein is entirely in keeping with the way they operate. And I have to say, that Indonesian bank set-up is brilliant."

"Brilliant or not, I want to confirm what Cameron has been telling me," Ava said.

"How can you do that?"

"If he has created a paper trail for the loans and real estate transactions, then everything should be on file at the bank. If I can access the records, I'll know who owns what and where, and maybe I can find a back door we can use to get our clients' money," she said. "When I finish speaking to you, I'm going to get what I need in the way of codes and passwords to get into the files, from Cameron."

"How long will that take?"

"If I have his passwords and I know where to look in the bank's database, no more than a few hours."

"Good — the more we know the better. But whether you get in or not, I do not want you to stay in Surabaya. I want you out of there today," Uncle said forcefully.

"Let me confirm what I've been told."

"Not if it means you cannot leave today."

"Uncle, if I can't get the information by noon, then there is something wrong with either me or the information."

"Call me back then."

"I will."

"And in the meantime, I'm going to hold a seat for you on a flight to Hong Kong. These are not people we should engage with, Ava. We need to get you far from them, and as quickly as we can."

"How about Perkasa?"

"You need to tell him what I said about the Italians. He is a good man. He knows how to keep his mouth shut. He also knows how to disappear," Uncle said.

"And the banker?"

"That will depend on what you find out," Uncle said carefully.

"I was thinking the same."

"We have some time," he said. "Discover what you can.

Meanwhile, I want to consider this thing in more detail. With these Italians, you cannot afford to make mistakes; you cannot afford to leave loose ends."

"Okay, I'll get the information I need and call you when I'm done."

"No later than noon," he said.

As Uncle put down the phone, the chill he'd felt earlier became a cold sweat. He had struggled not to sound panicked when he was speaking to Ava, but the moment she mentioned the 'Ndrangheta, panic had been his immediate reaction. The 'Ndrangheta were the most vicious and vengeful gangsters he knew of. When he had said to Ava that it hadn't turned out well when some triads tried to do business with them, that was an understatement. In one dispute over the quality of a drug shipment, the Italians had shot and killed five brothers, and then tortured and shot a deputy Mountain Master in front of his wife and daughter. The Triad Council considered launching a counterattack, but when an informer who knew the 'Ndrangheta told them the Italians would never back down and would fight to the last drop of their blood, the council decided it was wiser just to stop doing business with them.

Cameron now knows Ava. That thought burned in Uncle's head. If Cameron told the Italians, then getting her out of Surabaya wouldn't be enough to ensure her safety.

15

UNCLE'S CONVERSATION WITH AVA HAD GIVEN HIM A lot to think about, but before tackling those issues, he needed to reorganize his day. His first call was to Sonny.

"Yes, boss," Sonny answered.

"I won't be going to Sha Tin today. Ava might need my help with the job in Surabaya and I need to be reachable and not distracted in any way," Uncle said.

"Is there anything I can do?"

"Yes, but not right now. I'm going to book a flight to get her out of there today. I'll go with you to the airport to meet her. I'll let you know when to pick me up."

"Okay, I'll hang loose until I hear from you."

Uncle's next call was to the travel agency they had been using for ten years. Travel agencies in Hong Kong were disappearing, but out of loyalty Uncle continued to support theirs. Ten minutes later Ava had a first-class seat on a Cathay Pacific flight that left Surabaya at six p.m. If it left on time, it would land in Hong Kong at ten-thirty. Uncle phoned Sonny and told him to come to the apartment at nine-thirty.

With that settled, he was ready to think about Surabaya,

but as he looked around the apartment, Uncle felt confined and decided some fresh air might do him good. He slipped on his jacket, told Lourdes he was going out, and went downstairs to walk to the park. When he got there, he found an unoccupied bench and sat.

Why did it have to be the 'Ndrangheta? If it was any other organization, I could find a way around them. What are our options?

He returned to the fact that Cameron knew Ava's real name. The fact she had presented herself as working for Dynamic Financial Services didn't matter; that was a pretence that would quickly be exposed if the 'Ndrangheta pursued it. If pressured, the people at Dynamic would eventually tell the 'Ndrangheta absolutely everything they knew about Ava.

In addition to Dynamic, another way to get to Ava was through the friends of Johnny Yan she had met in Surabaya. Cameron would be sure to give up their names if he was questioned by his employers, and they would be as vulnerable to pressure as the accountants at Dynamic.

Uncle sighed. It seemed obvious that, although Ava was his priority, there were other people who would be at risk if Cameron talked. That made it even more necessary that Cameron be eliminated.

Uncle took a pack of Marlboros from his jacket and lit a stick. It was something he did reflexively, preoccupied as he was with the Cameron problem. He took three or four deep drags before he began to feel light-headed. He paused, gathered himself, and took one more drag. Cameron had to go, he told himself, but who should do it?

On their last job in Macau, the one in which Ava was shot

in the hip, she had executed a triad named Lok with a gun-shot to the head. Lok's death had been necessary for much the same reason Cameron's was going to be — namely, to let him live was to risk consequences that could be dangerous and far-reaching. Not consequences that might happen, but which were almost guaranteed. But despite the fact Ava had understood the necessity of killing Lok, Uncle realized it had taken an emotional toll on her. Did she still carry those psychological scars? And even if the logic was more compelling this time, could he ask her to kill again?

Uncle knew he could ask Perkasa to do it, but how would Ava react if he did? Would she think he didn't trust her? Would she think he'd gone behind her back? In all of the jobs they'd taken on, neither of them had made a decision this important without consulting their partner. Uncle lit another cigarette as he turned over his options. "Shit," he said, as he decided he had to let Ava make the call about who would take care of Cameron. But what he could also do was brief Perkasa and make sure he was there for backup. It wasn't an ideal solution, but it was practical.

The park was getting busy; there was a steady stream of people moving past and around Uncle in all directions. He barely noticed. His body may have been in Kowloon, but his mind was in Surabaya, and now he was considering how the 'Ndrangheta would respond if their bank manager was found dead. He was certain they wouldn't spare any effort trying to find out what had happened. They would start by retracing Cameron's steps for the previous few days, and if they did, what would they find? Had Cameron told anyone about the dinner with Johnny Yan's friends and Ava? Even if he hadn't, Westerners weren't that common in Surabaya.

Cameron and Yan's friends could have been easily noticed together, and that was another road that led to Ava.

So, killing Cameron wasn't enough. What they needed to do was find a way to shift the 'Ndrangheta's attention away from Ava and the people who had attended the dinner with Cameron. But what would it take to make that happen? As he contemplated that question, Uncle's phone rang.

"*Wei*," he answered.

"Uncle, this is Perkasa. Ava just left to go to the hotel to use her computer. She got passwords from Cameron. I'm assuming they're good."

"That's excellent news — and how is it going otherwise?"

"Well enough. I don't think I've ever worked with anyone as thorough or as tough as her. I could barely believe it when she charged up the cattle prod and used it to fry Cameron's balls, although I have to admit it was really effective."

"I don't need any more detail, but whatever she did, I'm sure she thought it was necessary," said Uncle, hiding his surprise at Ava's use of torture. "Did she tell you about our problem — about the 'Ndrangheta?"

"She did. It floored me. Who would have thought they'd be operating here, and on such a massive scale?"

"Do you understand how dangerous they are?"

"I have some idea," said Perkasa.

"If they find out about Ava, the locals she met, and you and the people you hired, nothing will stop them from coming after all of you."

"Are you saying that we need to get rid of Cameron?"

"I am."

"I was thinking the same thing, and I know Ava agrees," Perkasa said.

"I'll have to talk to her about who is going to do it. I'd prefer it be you, but I have to leave the decision with her. She has a strong sense of responsibility."

"You know I'll do whatever you want."

"Thanks, but if we kill him, we can't let the 'Ndrangheta find him."

"One of the men I hired has a farm. That's where we are now. We can bury Cameron somewhere where he'll never be found."

"Your man won't object to Cameron being buried in his backyard?"

"No, we'll just pay him more money."

"That's a good start, but I'm thinking what would be even better is if the 'Ndrangheta believe he's alive and has left Surabaya, taking their secrets with him. That would focus their attention on Cameron. In their minds, you and Ava wouldn't even exist."

"How could we do that?"

"I don't know yet, but we don't have a lot of time to come up with something if we are going to have both of you out of there today."

"I know."

"Tell me, these locals you hired — are they simply muscle, or are they more useful than that?"

"One is a police officer; the farmer is his brother. They are both capable and well connected."

"Would they have any influence at the airport?"

"I don't know, but I'll ask."

"Ask them now. I'll wait," said Uncle.

He lit a cigarette, found the taste increasingly more to his liking, and wondered if his body was returning to normal.

He finished the stick and was thinking of lighting another when Perkasa came on the line.

"They know a lot of people who work at the airport," he said. "For the right incentive, they tell me, all kinds of favours can be extracted."

"That is exactly what I was hoping to hear," Uncle said. "I have the germ of an idea, but I want to work on it a bit more before sharing the details. In the meantime, keep your local guys at hand, and let them know we're going to pay them very well for any additional help they provide."

"Will do," said Perkasa.

Uncle checked the time when he hung up. Assuming Cameron had given Ava accurate information — and why wouldn't he have, if an electric cattle prod was waiting for him? — Uncle figured that Ava would have accessed the bank's database by now. He was curious about what she was going to find. Even if it was only real estate deals, he wondered what their magnitude was and what the target markets were. There was also the question of Cameron's financial authority. Was he really limited to making transfers of a million dollars or less? If he wasn't, could Ava recoup the money their clients had lost? It would be dangerous, of course, since the Italians also had full access to the bank's database, and would be able to track any transfer authorized by Cameron.

Uncle stood and began a slow walk around the park. An idea was taking shape, and as it did his pace quickened. He lost track of how many times he went around the park before his phone rang again. He looked at it, saw Ava's number, and answered by saying, "I've been waiting to hear from you and it hasn't been easy."

"There was a lot of information to download, but as inter-esting as it is, I'm not sure it's of any benefit to us," she said. "Tell me what you have and then we'll decide together."

16

"THE 'NDRANGHETA HAVE BEEN BUYING REAL ESTATE from the day they took control of the bank," Ava said. "They started in Italy — in Rome, Milan, Florence, and Parma — and then their interest shifted to New York and Toronto. They aren't buying anything that would attract attention. Their focus has been on small office buildings, strip malls, small apartment complexes, that sort of thing. But when I did a rough estimate of the total value of their real estate holdings it came to more than five billion dollars."

"So that's how much cash they've flown into Surabaya?" Uncle asked.

"That would be my conclusion."

"That's more than I imagined," he said. "How much information is there about the real estate purchases?"

"Dates, company names, company officers and directors, addresses, and phone numbers for every company receiving a loan. Payment schedules, copies of corporate and personal guarantees — and on and on it goes, including detailed records of every property being financed."

"Just the kind of information you would need to record

if you were really running a banking operation."

"Exactly."

"And all of which would look completely above board unless someone knew what they were doing."

"Yes."

"How are the loans grouped?" Uncle asked.

"By branch and then by date, which makes for a simple paper trail. I downloaded all of the information twice. I'll keep a stick with me and arrange to have one sent to you before I leave Surabaya."

"You'll have to move quickly, because we have you booked on a Cathay Pacific flight leaving at six tonight."

"I'm at my hotel. They'll do it for me."

"Aside from the real estate information, did you find out anything else useful?"

"Yes, I looked at the bank's deposit records. At the outset, six years ago, large deposits were made about once a month. By year three, there were two or three a month, and over the last year it looks like cash has been flown in weekly. Also, for the past six months the deposits have typically been made on Wednesdays, which suggests to me the money is arriving on Tuesdays. I want to confirm that with Cameron."

"Are they chartering private planes?"

"Yes — a company called Brava Italia supplies them."

"How large are these weekly deposits?"

"None were smaller than the equivalent of twenty million U.S. dollars, and some exceeded fifty million."

"That's impressive," said Uncle, then he paused before asking, "Did you check on Cameron's ability to transfer money?"

"I tried, but I couldn't think of any way to confirm it

other than trying to send a wire transfer for more than a million. I didn't think that was wise, since it would have meant identifying a receiving bank, and even if I had been successful, it would have left a record."

"You did the right thing," Uncle said, not completely surprised that he and Ava had thought it through the same way. "Now, Ava, I've been doing a lot of thinking about what to do about Cameron. There is no doubt he's a major problem."

"I know, and something I forgot to say earlier is that he told me he meets the Italians every Sunday night at seven for dinner."

"If he goes tonight, what are the chances that he'll mention your name?"

"I'm one hundred percent certain he'd tell them that and a whole lot more."

"Then we have to make sure he never speaks to them," said Uncle.

He heard Ava sigh and knew she agreed with him, despite it being a heavy burden to bear.

"We have no choice," she said.

"But you don't have to be the one who does it," Uncle said. "I've discussed it with Perkasa, and he's prepared to do what's necessary."

"No," Ava said quickly. "You know I can't ask someone to do that kind of job for me."

"I know how you feel, but there is nothing more for you to prove, and no one will think less of you if you let Perkasa handle it."

"I can't," she said.

"Okay," he said, knowing there was no point in arguing with her. "But getting rid of Cameron doesn't eliminate the

'Ndrangheta threat. How do you think the Italians will react when Cameron doesn't show up for their meeting?"

"They'll go nuts. I imagine they'll talk to everyone in his immediate circle, and then try to reconstruct everything he's done and everyone he's met over the previous week."

"I agree, and that means there's a risk that your name and the names of Johnny Yan's friends will come up," said Uncle. "We need to give them a story that doesn't involve any of you."

"What do you have in mind?"

"Well, what if Cameron decided he'd had enough of life in Surabaya and it was time to leave? Given his experience with the 'Ndrangheta, he would know they would never let him leave voluntarily, so he'd have to sneak out of the country. He'd also need insurance, so I imagine he'd take all of the bank data with him in case the Italians managed to track him down."

"I like that as a story, but we'd need to provide proof for the Italians to believe it."

"Perkasa told me the guys working with you have connections at the airport. What if you bought an airline ticket in Cameron's name using one of his credit cards for a flight out of Indonesia, and what if someone pretending to be Cameron actually checked in at the airport and — even better — got on the flight?"

Ava hesitated, and Uncle wondered if his idea was too far-fetched.

Then she said, "That might work, you know. I could get Cameron to call his housekeeper and tell her he's taking a short, unexpected trip out of the country and needs his passport and an overnight bag. Perkasa could pick them up from her. For sure, she'd be one of the first people the Italians would speak to when he didn't show for dinner. That would plant the idea that he's left Surabaya and point them towards the airport. We could park his car there for them to find."

"Is all of that doable?"

"Entirely. In fact, I have his wallet with me and could book a flight right now. Where do you want him to go?"

Uncle smiled. "He's scheduled to meet the Italians at seven, so why don't you find a flight that leaves around that time and book it. The destination doesn't matter."

"You mentioned him getting on a flight; how would we arrange that?" Ava asked.

"Talk to Perkasa about that. Hopefully, with enough money and his connections, we'll find airline employees willing to turn a blind eye if someone else uses Cameron's passport."

"Someone else?"

"Why not Perkasa? We want to get him out of Surabaya as well."

"I'll talk to him before booking a flight for Cameron. His men may have better connections at a specific airline over another, and if that's the case then I'll book the flight on it."

"You are as logical as ever," Uncle said.

"Thanks, but as much as I like that we've cobbled together a plan, I hate the idea of leaving Surabaya without recovering a single dollar for our clients."

"Your safety is my priority."

"I know," Ava said. "I'll be on that plane at six."

"Do you want me to brief Perkasa?"

"No, I'll handle it."

"Fine. Call me if you run into any problems. Otherwise

I will be at Chek Lap Kok to meet you when your flight arrives," he said.

"We'll make it work."

"Be careful, Ava."

"As always."

Uncle put down the phone feeling confident that Ava and Perkasa would execute things smoothly in Surabaya. Then he sat back and thought about the information Ava had unearthed. It had to be of value, but to whom? And how could they extract enough value to make their clients whole?

Under normal circumstances, the information could be used as leverage to pry money from those who had stolen it. But in this case that was the 'Ndrangheta, and there was no way he was going near them. Who else was there who might have an interest in the information? One group came immediately to mind, but would they be willing to pay for it? And even if they were, would they be prepared to pay millions? Uncle knew one man who might be able to answer those questions, and he picked up the phone to call him.

Zhang Delun had spent his entire working life with the Hong Kong Police Force, and had reached the rank of Chief Superintendent before retiring. He and Uncle had shared information and collaborated countless times over the years. It had been a tightly held, very confidential relationship that had never been breached. They weren't friends, but they had developed a sense of mutual trust and respect that went beyond friendship. Uncle hadn't spoken to Zhang in years, and as he dialled his number it occurred to him that something may have happened to the policeman. But a moment later he felt a touch of relief when he heard a familiar voice say, "*Wei*, this is Zhang."

"How are you, Zhang? This is Uncle."

"Uncle, what could a retired triad boss want from a retired chief superintendent?"

"I'm calling for your advice. I have stumbled across some information that doesn't involve triads or the Hong Kong police, but could be of real interest to other law enforcement agencies. I'd like to know how best to handle it."

17

UNCLE DID NOT HEAR FROM AVA FOR THE REST OF afternoon, so he phoned Perkasa at quarter to six.

"Uncle, I was hoping to hear from you," the jago answered.

"And I'm glad I caught you. Did things go well?" Uncle asked. "Is Ava at the airport?"

"She boarded her plane five minutes ago. I'm boarding mine soon."

"So everything went well?"

"Cameron is dead, and buried where no one will find him. His car is parked at the airport, and I'm sitting at a Singapore Airlines gate with his passport and a boarding pass to Singapore in his name. Nearby is a very co-operative and helpful gate agent who — if asked — will swear that he saw Cameron get on this plane. My local guys really came through for us."

"That's good to hear. I was worried," said Uncle. "How did it go with Cameron? Did Ava take care of him?"

"No, she didn't have to."

"What do you mean?"

"We think he had a heart attack. One of my men found

him keeled over. He was tied to a chair and had been sitting in the sun. We think the heat, the picana, and the stress got to him."

Uncle took a deep breath. "That was fortunate. I didn't relish the idea of one of you having to put a bullet in his head."

"Ava and I felt the same sense of relief."

"What are your plans now?"

"When I get to Singapore, I'll clear customs and immigration under my own name, stay overnight somewhere, then catch a flight to Jakarta tomorrow."

"That sounds perfect," said Uncle. "Perkasa, I can't thank you enough for your help with all of this."

"You've done enough for my family over the years. I was pleased I was able to help."

"Still, I'm going to send you more money tomorrow, and I don't want you to argue with me about that," Uncle said. "If you think it is too much, give some of it to your contacts in Surabaya."

"Ava already looked after them very well, but it wouldn't hurt to sweeten the deal."

"I agree, and now I'll let you catch that plane. Give my regards to your father."

Uncle put down the phone and felt a slight tremor in his right hand. He stared at the hand and realized he had been nervous about the call to Perkasa. It seemed things had gone perfectly, but in the back of his mind he had been prepared for the worst.

He had a few hours to wait before Sonny would arrive, and he wondered how best to spend the time. After talking back and forth with Zhang for more than an hour, he phoned Fanling and laid his bets on the afternoon races at

Sha Tin, and then he took a nap that went longer than he expected. The nap refreshed him, and it also seemed to settle his stomach. He thought about going out for something to eat, and then decided a bowl of plain white rice would suffice. If he still felt well when he met Ava, they could go out for a late-night plate of noodles.

Fifteen minutes later, and with a bowl of rice in his lap, Uncle sat in his chair and watched reruns of the day's races. They were shown in real time which meant there was a break between each race, and when the last race ended it was already past nine o'clock. Uncle freshened up in the bathroom, put on his suit jacket, and went downstairs to wait for Sonny.

Traffic was light and they made it to Chep Lap Kok thirty minutes before Ava's plane was scheduled to land. Sonny parked in the VIP lane directly outside the arrivals area, and as Uncle was getting out a policeman hurried over.

"You can't park —" the policeman began to say, then stopped when he saw Uncle and Sonny. "Uncle, it is a pleasure to see you again." He then put a fist inside his opposite palm, lowered his head, and moved his hands up and down in a gesture of respect.

Uncle acknowledged him with a nod and said, "Thank you for your courtesy. I assume my car and driver can wait here for me?"

"*Momentai, momentai,* Uncle."

Uncle entered the cavernous arrivals hall, bought a late-edition newspaper, and went to the Kit Kat Koffee House. Even late on a Sunday evening the hall was bustling, and there was a wall of people lined up near the exit doors waiting for loved ones to emerge, something Uncle never did. The

Kit Kat was his normal waiting place, and when Ava arrived she would know where to find him.

He ordered a cup of coffee and a glass of water and spread his paper on the retro-style laminated table. When his drinks were served, he took a cigarette from his pack, and was about to light it when he noticed the server staring at him and pointing at a sign that said no smoking. Uncle put away his lighter, but between sips of coffee he held the cigarette between his lips.

He read the racing writer's analysis of that day's races and didn't find much to disagree with. He then turned to the news section and slowly worked his way through the paper. He was focused on a story about Chinese investment in Africa when he sensed he wasn't alone. He looked up and saw Ava standing in front of him. "My beautiful girl," he said as he rose to his feet.

She leaned forward and kissed him on the forehead. "I'm so happy you came to meet me."

Uncle hesitated, not sure how to react. What she said wasn't unusual, but her voice had cracked ever so slightly, and her tone seemed uncertain. He looked more closely at her and thought her face was paler than normal. "Is everything all right? Did something happen that you haven't told me?" he asked.

She blinked, then averted her eyes.

Something did happen, he thought.

"No, nothing happened. Things with Cameron went as planned — in fact a bit better than planned," she said.

Uncle began to speak again but caught himself. If there was something she wasn't telling him, he knew she would have her reasons. "Well then, let's go. Sonny has the car parked at the VIP curb. We got here early, so I'm sure the police are growing impatient with us," he said, and reached for one of her bags.

"No, Uncle, I can manage," she said.

As they began to walk towards the terminal exit, he said, "I booked you a suite in the Mandarin Oriental, and I would have taken you to dinner at Man Wah but it closes at ten."

"Just as well — they can fuss at Man Wah, and I'm not in the mood for a fuss. I'd rather eat noodles."

He slipped his hand around her forearm and squeezed. "Then noodles it will be. The restaurant I like that's close to the Mandarin is open until two."

"I would like to shower and change before we eat if that's not a bother."

"There's no rush," he said.

Half an hour later, Sonny stopped the Mercedes at the front door of the Mandarin. The talk en route had been casual, with Uncle asking about her family, and Ava telling him about Amanda and Michael's plans to marry. She then explained at length her role in the wedding party, and her doubts about how well she could pull it off. Uncle found that rather strange. Usually, when a job went sideways as this one had, Ava was eager to pick apart the details. Now it seemed to be the furthest thing from her mind.

He waited in the hotel lobby while she checked in, showered, and changed. He smiled when he saw her emerge from the elevator with a face that had more colour and in a mood that seemed more buoyant.

It was now well past eleven o'clock, but the streets in Central were still crowded. Sunday was family day for the Chinese, the traditional day off for the hundreds of thousands of Filipina housemaids and *yayas* who lived in Hong Kong, and just another workday for the restaurants and businesses that stayed open to serve them. Uncle looped his arm through Ava's and let her navigate their way to the noodle restaurant.

The owner saw them as they reached the entrance, and before a world was spoken, he was already moving other customers around so he could accommodate them. Most of the other tables were occupied by families having a late-night snack. At one, four heavily tattooed men, two of them with their hair pulled back in ponytails, were drinking beer and sharing platters of grilled squid and snow pea tips fried in oil and garlic. When the men saw Uncle and Ava, they began to talk among themselves, and then stood as one to approach the table.

"It is an honour to meet you, Uncle," the one who looked the oldest said, bowing his head. The others followed suit.

"Where are you from?" Uncle asked.

"14K Wanchai."

"Give my regards to Mountain Master Chen," said Uncle.

"And he would want to send his deepest regards to you," the man said.

"Thank you," Uncle said, with a slight dip of his head.

The man stared at Ava. "Are you Ava Lee?"

"I am," she said, taken aback.

"Everyone has heard about Macau," he said.

"You're famous now," another added.

Ava lowered her eyes, embarrassed and confused.

The men hovered for a moment, and then bowed to Uncle again before returning to their table.

"You have become something of a legend," Uncle said with a slight smile.

"For what? Storming a house and shooting an unarmed man? That was hardly a contribution to mankind."

"Every society has its own morality, its own code of ethics."

"I never thought I was part of that society," Ava said.

Her tone was sharp, and her remark surprised Uncle. "You are a brave girl, Ava. Just think of it in that light," he said softly.

"I don't feel so brave about the way I left Surabaya," she said.

"There was no other choice."

"I wonder if our clients would look at it that way."

"They may not have to," Uncle said.

Ava looked across the table at him, and he knew he had captured her attention. "What are you talking about?" she asked.

"Why don't we order our food before we discuss business," he said as the owner arrived.

When their order of noodles and beef in XO sauce, steamed broccoli with oyster sauce, jasmine tea for Ava, and a San Miguel for Uncle was in, Ava leaned towards him. "What did you mean earlier? Are you saying there might still be a way to help them?"

"There is a possibility. It's not a certainty, but not all of our doors are closed."

18

"AFTER WE TALKED EARLIER TODAY, I DID SOME THINK-ing and made some phone calls," Uncle began as their drinks arrived. "I spoke to an old friend on the Hong Kong Police Force, and he put me on to a mutual friend in the Security Bureau. Men I trust, you understand. Men I really trust."

"Men you trust," Ava repeated as she sipped her tea.

Uncle took a deep swig of his beer. "I mentioned the 'Ndrangheta to them, and that piqued their interest. When I explained — very generally — what you had uncovered, they became quite excited. I then put a proposal to them, and while their reaction was not exactly what I expected, it was close enough to make things interesting," he said, taking another pull of beer.

Their food arrived: a huge platter of noodles, slivers of beef piled high, almost glittering under the combination of XO sauce and overhead lighting. The owner stood to one side, admiring his kitchen's handiwork. This wasn't a normal serving, Uncle knew — maybe not even a normal *double* serving. And the ratio of beef to noodles was outlandish. Uncle nodded his thanks and said, "I will have another beer."

"Should you?" Ava asked, and then looked slightly guilty.

"It is that kind of night," he said, and then wondered what had prompted her question.

They dug into the noodles. Uncle filled his bowl, extracted a sliver of beef, and held it in the air, examining it. His second beer arrived before he finished his first mouthful. "We may not have to abandon our clients," he said, as he set the empty beer bottle to one side and picked up the new one. "At least, that is the message I got from my friends."

"I don't understand," Ava said, eating as vigorously as Uncle.

"The information you got from the bank — it has value."

"Value to whom? Are you suggesting that we blackmail the Italians?"

"Of course not. We need to stay far away from the Italians. The information, according to my friends, has the greatest value to the police. They think — in fact they are convinced — that we should be able to sell it to a police organization."

"Why would the Hong Kong police have any interest?" Ava asked.

"Evidently everyone is interested in the 'Ndrangheta, although not that much is known about them. There was an assumption among the Hong Kong police that they are not that well organized. When I started to talk about the bank, about the transfers, and about the real estate, it intrigued my friends. They thought — and they told me the assumption is commonplace — that the 'Ndrangheta was a hundred or so loosely knit families. They had no idea there was this kind of structure to them."

"And they are willing to pay for the information we have?"

"No, not them. They said we need to talk to the police

forces in the countries where they are operating — Italy, of course, and then Indonesia, Venezuela, the U.S., and Canada."

Ava poured herself more tea and said, "Even assuming we do have something worth paying for, how do we keep the information secure?"

"Do you mean how do we keep the 'Ndrangheta from finding out who passed on the information about the bank, the cash, the real estate holdings, and — probably the most important thing of all — the people and companies whose names are attached to those transactions?"

"Exactly."

"Yes, that is the problem."

"And a big one," said Ava. "I wouldn't feel safe giving information to anyone in Italy, Indonesia, or Venezuela, and when I say anyone, I mean *anyone*. The U.S. makes me almost as uncomfortable, unless you know someone there you trust as much as you trust your friends here."

"The problem in the U.S. is you would have to involve so many different security organizations. With all that overlapping bureaucracy, it's difficult to get a decision made, and it is even tougher to keep things quiet. I'm not suggesting they could be bought, but with all of the competing jurisdictions it could get sloppy. And we don't need sloppy."

"So where does that leave us?" Ava asked.

"Canada."

"Aside from the fact I live there, what else recommends Canada?"

"It was not my idea actually; it came from my friend."

"Does he know about me?"

"No, I've never mentioned you by name. But I did explain

a little about our clients, and about the bank's involvement in Toronto. That's when he said the Mounties should be contacted. He spoke highly of them — one force, acting independently, less chance of breaches. And that is where our clients live, so it would be logical. Also, I believe it wouldn't be far-fetched to ask for the money our clients lost as compensation for providing them with the information."

"So, our story is that we're simply seeking justice for our Canadian clients, not trying to extort money for information."

"That's true enough, is it not?"

"In a rough way, yes, but are you suggesting we put a price tag of thirty million dollars on that justice?"

"Why not try? All they can say is no."

Uncle watched as Ava nibbled some broccoli and sipped her tea. He knew her well enough to understand that she was thinking through the proposal, weighing their options, and spinning out various scenarios.

Finally, she looked at him and said, "I know some Mounties."

"I remembered that you do."

"That doesn't mean I'd trust any of them with our lives."

"How do you figure?"

"If we pass along this information and the Italians find out we were the source, they'll kill us."

"No," Uncle said, putting down his chopsticks and trying to ignore a cramp in his belly. "What I mean is, why do you think these men might not be trustworthy?"

Ava shrugged. "The Royal Canadian Mounted Police are as much a big government bureaucracy as they are a police force. It's unrealistic to think they'd consider handing over thirty million dollars without some kind of committee getting involved, and without their doing due diligence on us and on our information."

"Are you concerned about the quality of the information?"

"Not in the least," she said.

"Then it comes down to personal credibility and trust."

"I know."

He reached across the table and placed his hand on hers. "The only way I think this will work is if you can find one person you can really trust, and you deal only with that one person. Whoever it is has to respect and maintain your anonymity and keep you completely isolated. They have to be your shield. Is there a Mountie you trust that much?"

"Perhaps."

"You would have to be very careful about how you approach them and what you say initially. You could share part of the truth. No names at the start, just a sort of general outline, but with enough bait to see if they are willing to be enticed," he said, and then stopped when he realized he was lecturing. The last thing Ava needed from him was instructions on how to talk to a contact.

"Uncle, I'd rather do the parsing myself until the level of interest can be gauged. I mean, I do think I can trust my contact, but I still need to confirm how much."

"Of course, that is wise," he said, feeling slightly lightheaded and wishing he hadn't ordered a second beer.

"One step at a time, eh? That's what you taught me."

He started to respond when the cramp in his stomach suddenly felt like teeth gnawing at his innards. He sat back, his eyes watering as he raised them towards the ceiling. He took several deep breaths and the pain started to ebb. "How soon do you think you can make contact?" he asked finally.

"It's Sunday morning there. My contact won't be at work, but I have a private number. I'll call when I get back to the hotel. But, Uncle, I'm really nervous about this. You're so right when you say we need maximum distance between the information and ourselves. And you know, an idea just came to me that might help us achieve that," she said. "Tell me, could we open a numbered bank account with your friends at the Kowloon Light and Power Bank?"

"Of course."

"But could we open one that was easy to trace — one that anyone with any savvy could find their way into and locate the account holder?"

"Why would we do that?"

"I would want the name Andy Cameron attached to the account."

Uncle smiled. "Even after all these years, you can still surprise me with that wonderful mind of yours, Ava."

"So, you think Cameron can open an account there?"

"He most definitely can, and that might offer us an extra twist," he said. "What if you told the Mountie you were representing Cameron, and that he was the person looking to sell the information?"

"That makes perfect sense," she said after a slight hesitation. "He's on the run. He can't work again so he needs money to secure his future and keep himself out of the reach of the 'Ndrangheta."

"Exactly. It is a story that hangs together very well."

Ava nodded. "If we can get everything else to fall into place, the Kowloon Light and Power Bank may just have acquired a new client."

They left the restaurant without paying for the meal. The owner had refused to give a bill to Uncle, and after a few moments of protest, Uncle thanked him and left a HK$500 tip.

The streets had calmed down. It was getting too late for families, but it was still too early for the nightclubs and karaoke bars to begin losing customers. They walked downhill towards the Mandarin, Uncle's arm again looped through Ava's. They had only walked about half the distance when he felt another sharp pain in his stomach. He stopped walking and took a deep breath, hoping he could get Ava back to the hotel without incident.

He saw her looking at him and tried to act normal, but the pain became even more intense and he lurched towards the street, bent over. Ava reached out to give him support, but he waved her off. Then he coughed, took a couple of rapid breaths, and threw up on the road. His stomach heaved, and he threw up again, and then again until his stomach was empty. His body still ached, and he was covered in a cold sweat, but gradually he began to regain some measure of control.

Ava stood at his side, gently holding his arm. "My God, Uncle, what is that?" she asked, pointing down at the road.

Uncle looked at the remnants of his dinner on the street. The noodles were streaked with blood. He wiped at his mouth with his jacket sleeve and shook his head, trying to clear it. "I'm afraid I cannot handle spicy food anymore," he said.

"Wait here. I'm going to that 7-Eleven over there," Ava said.

Uncle leaned against a wall and watched her disappear into the store. A few minutes later she came out with a bottle of water and a sleeve of tissues. She opened the water and passed it to him. He sipped lightly, no more than wetting his lips.

She took out a tissue and gently patted his sweating brow. "I'm worried about you, Uncle," she said.

"No reason to be. I'm just an old man having an old man's aches and pains."

"Uncle, you would tell me if it was more than that, wouldn't you?"

"Of course," he lied.

He held her arm the rest of the way to the hotel. Neither of them spoke until they saw Sonny standing by the Mercedes. "I will go straight home. You call me after you talk to your Mountie," he said.

"I'm not sure I'll reach him tonight, but I'll try. If I do, you'll hear from me."

"Good. One way or another, we need to close this case. We owe it to our clients to do the best we can for them."

"Yes, Uncle, we owe it to our clients," she said.

Uncle slid into the back seat of the car, and noticed Ava speaking to Sonny intensely. Neither of them looked in his direction, but he knew she was telling Sonny about what had just happened in the street. It had been silly of him to test his stomach like that. Thinking back, it was inevitable that two beers and all that rich food would prove to be more than he could handle. Back to white rice and congee for a while, he thought.

Sonny didn't say anything when he got into the driver's seat, but Uncle sensed he was itching to and decided to head him off. "I'm going straight to the apartment, and let's keep it quiet as we go. It has been a long day, and I'm tired."

19

WHEN UNCLE WOKE THE FOLLOWING MORNING, HE didn't get out of bed immediately, but lay quietly thinking about the events of the previous night and gauging the damage he'd done to his body. There was no doubt he had gone overboard with beer and food. Well, he figured, that was a lesson learned.

He swung his feet over the side of the bed and pushed himself to his feet. He seemed steady enough and his stomach wasn't at war with him. *So far, so good*, he thought, and headed for the bathroom. It was just past seven o'clock, and obviously Ava hadn't phoned during the night or Lourdes would have woken him. Had things gone badly with the Mountie? He turned around and walked to the phone in the living room. He checked it for messages, found none, and called Ava's cell number. His call went directly to voicemail.

"This is Uncle. I'm just wondering how it went last night with the Mountie," he said. "Call me when you can."

It had to have gone well, he tried to convince himself as he headed once more towards the bathroom. Ava was too persuasive for it to have gone otherwise.

After dressing, Uncle asked Lourdes to prepare some white rice, and while she went about that he left the apartment to buy his newspapers and the racing form for Happy Valley.

On his return, he leafed through the newspapers and managed to eat and keep down a half bowl of rice. There was still no word from Ava, and he was thinking of calling her again when he remembered he had promised her he would set up a bank account for Andy Cameron at the Kowloon Light and Power Bank. He phoned the bank — in which the triads had partial ownership — and was put through to the president, Henry Cheng. Uncle and Cheng had done much business together over the years.

"Uncle, it has been a long time since we talked. What can I do for you?"

"I want to open an account."

"Another one?"

"It isn't for me. I want you to open an account in the name of Andy Cameron."

Cheng hesitated. "Is he a Hong Kong resident?"

"No."

"Does he have a local address, a Hong Kong ID number, or is he registered with the Department of Inland Revenue?"

"No."

"That makes it difficult."

"But, I trust, not impossible," said Uncle.

"Are you comfortable telling me why you want to open this account? That might help me find a solution."

"You know I trust you, Henry, but this information can't be shared with anyone else," said Uncle.

"You know it won't be."

"All right — if things go as planned, a substantial amount of money will be put into that account, and from there will be redistributed to clients of mine from whom it was stolen," said Uncle. "I want to be able to control the distribution without having my name attached to the account, and if anyone pokes into it, the only name I want them to find is that of Andy Cameron."

"That is an interesting challenge," said Cheng. "I think there is a way we can do it, but it would mean you putting even more trust in me."

"Explain."

"I am allowed to open accounts in the bank's name as trust accounts. We have done it from time to time, in situations, for example, when someone with an account here dies suddenly and doesn't leave a will. We transfer those funds to a new account in the bank's name that is in trust for the estate of the deceased. In this case, the account could be Kowloon Light and Power account number xxxx, in trust for the estate of Andy Cameron. I would have the authority to release funds, and of course I would only do so at your direction. Does that work? It would imply that Cameron was dead."

"It could also imply that's what he wants people to think, which is good," said Uncle. "I have another question for you. When the time comes to distribute the money, could I authorize the transfers by sending you a letter signed by Andy Cameron? That way you would have something to show if you were ever asked about it."

"Will I be asked?'"

"I doubt it, but if you are, your back will be covered."

"Then I don't object to getting written instructions from

Andy Cameron. But please call me and give me a heads-up before you send anything with his name. And make sure you send it directly to me. I don't wish to confuse my staff."

"Thank you, Henry. I should know in the next day or two if any of this is going to happen, but I would appreciate it if you could set up the account today in anticipation of our success."

"I'll call you with the details."

The arrangement with the bank was a bit more complicated than Uncle had envisioned, but as long as Henry Cheng was comfortable with it, then so was he.

Uncle checked the time and decided he could try Ava again. But once more he was sent straight to voicemail.

"I wanted to let you know that I've made arrangements with Kowloon Light and Power Bank for an account in Andy Cameron's name," he said.

Uncle returned to his newspapers as a way of passing time, but he was finding it harder not to feel anxious about Ava's silence. He waited for almost another hour before reaching for the phone one more time. As he did, it rang.

"*Wei*," he answered.

"Sorry to call so late," Ava said in a rush. "I just woke up. I was up half the night negotiating with the Mounties."

"I understand," Uncle said more calmly than he felt. "So, where are we?"

"First of all, how are you feeling? You really scared me last night."

"I'm fine. As I said, I have to be more careful about what I eat these days."

"Please make sure that you do," she said. "I can't bear to see you like that."

"There is nothing to worry about," Uncle said. "Now, I'm anxious to know how it went with the Mounties."

"It did not go exactly as planned, although I think it went well enough," she said. "My contact agreed to help, but after he contacted his superiors, they insisted on knowing who I was. I told my contact that I wouldn't use my own name, but that I sometimes used the name Jennie Kwong. He asked if it was legitimate, and when I told him I had a real Hong Kong passport and ID card in that name, he agreed to present me to them as such."

"So your discussion with them was conducted through your contact?"

"So far, that's how it has been."

"And you think it went well?"

"I think it went okay, but I'm waiting for a final answer. I told them we were representing the person who had the information, and that he wanted thirty million for it. They said they couldn't agree to pay anything until they had verified the information was accurate and of value. Uncle, they also insisted on a name. I had to give them Cameron's and the name of the bank, and I provided them with a sample of our information. I gave them twenty-four hours to get back to us. If they don't, I told them we'd walk away and open talks with the Americans."

"Using the Americans as leverage was clever."

"Well, I figured what we have provides the Mounties with an opportunity to make a real splash in international policing. I'm sure they wouldn't want to see the Americans get the credit for something they could have had for themselves."

"I agree, but I wish you didn't have to give them Cameron's name quite so soon," Uncle said.

"I pushed back, but they were so insistent that I didn't think I had a choice. But in any case, why not? As far as anyone knows he flew from Surabaya to Singapore early yesterday evening. I told them he was in hiding."

"Well, it is true they have no way to disprove any of that," said Uncle. "Did you get my message about opening an account in Cameron's name?"

"I did, so the money going in will be attached to him, but are the final recipients going to be identifiable when it leaves?"

"No. After it reaches Cameron's account, we will make sure it begins a remarkable journey that no one will be able to follow. That is assuming, of course, that we can conclude a deal. What do you think of our chances?"

"Uncle, I have no idea. It isn't really about the information being accurate or not. It is all a question of what actual value the Mounties ascribe to it."

"Still, I like the way we are going about it, and I have to say it is quite an ingenious approach."

"What — asking the Canadian government to pay us thirty million dollars so we can reimburse Canadian citizens who lost that money in the first place because they were trying to avoid paying taxes?" said Ava.

"That too," Uncle laughed. "Though I meant using a dead man as the vehicle."

Uncle heard Ava mutter something unrecognizable, and then she said, "Uncle, I want to apologize if I seem rude, but I really need to go to the bathroom."

"Go ahead." He laughed again. "We will talk later."

"I might go for a run as well, but I'll take my phone with me in case the Mounties call."

"I'll be here. I have no plans, but I have to say that I hope they call sooner rather than later. I'm not as good at waiting as I used to be."

When his phone went silent, Uncle sat back in his chair and replayed his conversation with Ava. They had made progress, of that he was certain, but he couldn't imagine the Mounties — or anyone else for that matter — would agree to hand over thirty million dollars based on a few pages of information. They would ask for more, he expected, and maybe more again. Then, even if they were satisfied the information was real, Uncle was certain they would try to haggle about the price. *We should have given ourselves some wiggle room by asking for more than thirty million*, he thought, and then almost instantly another idea came to him. *Could the solution be that simple?* he wondered, and then said aloud, "Yes, yes, yes, it could work."

He reached for the phone to call Ava, and then stopped. He should wait until she heard from the Mounties before adding another complication to her negotiations.

His phone rang. He picked it up, and without thinking said, "Ava?"

"You aren't as fortunate as that," his old friend Fong said.

"Sorry, Ava and I have been doing a lot of chatting. The job we're on is heating up."

"Does it have you completely tied up for the day?"

"No, but I should be available if she calls," said Uncle.

"I have to come to Hong Kong for a short meeting with Sammy Wing," Fong said, referring to the Mountain Master of Wanchai. "I was hoping you could meet me for lunch and then join me for a relaxing few hours at a massage parlour I've been frequenting. You won't have any trouble using your mobile phone."

"Is there a particular reason for this unexpected invitation?" Uncle asked.

"Yes, I would like to spend some time with my oldest and closest friend, but other than that, no."

"I'm not so sure about lunch. My stomach is still acting up."

"A massage shouldn't upset it," said Fong.

"I guess not, and I could use a bit of relaxation," Uncle said. "So, yes, I'll join you at the massage parlour. What's it called?"

"Magic Touch. It's in Central, across the street from the Shanghai Tang store."

"What time?"

"How does one o'clock work for you?"

"That's fine, I'll see you then."

Uncle rarely went to massage parlours anymore. In fact, he couldn't remember the last time he had frequented one. When he was in Fanling he used to go about once a month, and always when he was feeling stressed. Fong was correct that a good massage could be relaxing, and Uncle knew he could use some of that right now.

20

UNCLE'S MASSEUSE WAS A PLUMP, MIDDLE-AGED woman with a broad smile who asked him what level of intensity he wanted her to exert. He told her to be gentle, and she not only tried to be, but kept checking in with him to make sure he was comfortable.

The first round of massage lasted forty-five minutes, and then Uncle joined Fong in a steam room. They were scheduled for thirty minutes, but after fifteen, Uncle began to feel drained and left. He sat wrapped in a bathrobe in an easy chair in the lounge while he waited for the continuation of his massage. His phone had been on and near him except for when he was in the steam room. It hadn't rung, and there were no messages on it.

The massage had relaxed him, but now as he sat in the chair he began to worry about Ava's progress. He assumed she had been negotiating with the Mounties, and if that was the case, then he was surprised she didn't have some idea of what they were prepared to offer. Maybe they had decided to play tough; to test the reality of a twenty-four-hour deadline; to confirm that Ava was actually prepared to walk away from them and go to the Americans. If they had, they'd find out quickly enough that Ava didn't make idle threats.

Uncle's masseuse entered the lounge and motioned for him to rejoin her in her cubicle. He lay on the table face down, and felt her fingers begin to knead his shoulder muscles.

"Your muscles have become tenser," she said. "The steam room should have had the opposite effect."

"I have things on my mind," he said.

"Let them go."

Uncle closed his eyes and tried to concentrate on the massage. Gradually his mind stopped turning in circles, and as he felt himself begin to drift off, his phone rang. The masseuse handed it to him with a slight look of impatience on her face.

"*Wei*," said Uncle.

"This is Ava."

"Excuse me, but I have to take this call in private," he said to the masseuse. "Will you leave, or shall I?"

"It is easier if I go."

"I can talk now," Uncle said to Ava after a moment.

"We need to speak quickly. The clock is ticking."

"I'm all ears."

"I am — or at least Jennie Kwong is — now dealing directly with two senior officers in the RCMP. My contact has been taken out of the loop," she said. "They've been looking into the information I gave them, and they tell me the transactions are supported by such a complex structure that they need more time to complete their investigation."

"Did they say what they think about what they've found so far?"

"They think Bank Linno is certainly very suspicious, as is Andy Cameron's involvement," she said. "And by the way, they confirmed that Cameron flew from Surabaya to Singapore on Sunday. When I told them not to bother looking for him there because he had already left, they said they hoped so because his trail was rather obvious."

"How much more time did they ask for?"

"An unspecified number of days."

"I don't think we should agree to that, but what do you think?" he asked.

"The way I see it, the longer this gets stretched out, the greater the risk. The Italians must know by now that Cameron has gone to Singapore, and they'll assume he's done a runner. I'm sure they're doing everything they can to track him down."

"But they'll never find him."

"True, but my fear is that in a few days they might start asking his friends where he went," she said. "The last thing I want is for their attention to switch back to Surabaya. We don't want them talking to people at the airport or trying to find out who Cameron met with in the days before he disappeared."

"I think our best chance to get our clients some money and to get distance from this entire affair is to push for a quick resolution. What surprises me is that they haven't insisted on meeting with Cameron."

"That, I think, will be next," said Ava.

"And if they do, how do we respond? Do we end it?"

"No, I want that money. But I'm beginning to think that what I want even more is for every law enforcement agency in the countries where the bank was doing business to begin hounding the 'Ndrangheta. I want the Italians to be focused on fending off that attack, and not chasing the ghost of Andy Cameron. A good offence is often the best defence."

"Are you prepared to make the information we have available to all of them free of charge?"

"If it comes down to that, yes I am — as long as we can do it anonymously."

"I agree. The priority has to be securing everyone's safety," Uncle said. "But the deadline you gave the Mounties still has a few hours before it expires, yes?"

"Yes, but if they won't change their position what does that matter?"

"Do you think they might change their minds if we didn't ask them to pay us the thirty million with Canadian taxpayer money, and instead asked them to help us get the money in another way?"

"What are you suggesting?" Ava asked.

"I'm thinking about the airplane full of cash that the banker said arrives every Tuesday in Surabaya."

He heard Ava take a deep breath and knew he had struck a chord.

Before she could speak, he continued: "I've been mulling this over all day. If the plane is seized when it lands, it will provide proof positive that money laundering is going on; it would take the Indonesian-based Italians right out of the game; and it would give the Mounties the money to pay us. But before any of that could happen, you would have to confirm when the plane will be arriving in Surabaya."

"I would have to talk to the Mounties, and they would have to have conversations with the Indonesians," Ava said with an edge of excitement in her voice — a sign to Uncle that she was already on board with the idea. "Flight plans have to be filed. Planes can't just arrive unexpectedly at an airport."

"You told me earlier that you thought people at the Indonesian airport were being paid off."

"That doesn't mean air traffic control. All we need to know is that a Brava Italia plane is scheduled to land in Surabaya tomorrow," she said. "Mind you, this can't be done without some level of Indonesian involvement. I can stress to the Mounties how compromised Indonesian Customs are, and ask them to find another way to get the information that won't alert the Italians."

"I also can't see that plane being seized without the involvement of the Indonesian police. Do you think the Mounties have strong enough connections in Jakarta to make that happen?"

"If they don't, we'll know soon enough."

"Ava, what have you told them about the planes?"

"Absolutely nothing."

"Good. You'll have the element of surprise in your favour. Hopefully you can spur them into action."

"Uncle, are you sure you want to do this with tomorrow's flight?" Ava asked.

"Yes. We can't afford to wait another week."

"What if they can't organize things that quickly? What if they reject the entire idea?"

"What is there to organize? We're talking about a small commercial jet with only a flight crew, which is being met, as far as we can tell, by a small crew of local Italians. We don't need an army to seize it."

"But what if the Mounties can't make it work?"

"Then we should send them, and the American and

Italian governments, all the information we have on the 'Ndrangheta, and walk away."

"I can only hope that if we get to that point, the 'Ndrangheta will focus on defending themselves and not be so concerned about who provided the authorities with that information."

"If and when it comes time to send it, we'll find a way to make sure Andy Cameron is fingered."

Ava sighed. "This has been such a difficult case," she said, and then added abruptly, "Uncle, the Mounties are calling. I have to go."

"Call me when you have things sorted out with them one way or another. I won't be able to relax until I know where we stand."

21

AFTER THEIR MASSAGES, UNCLE TURNED DOWN FONG'S invitation to go out for something to eat. When Ava called, he wanted to be in the calm environment of his apartment. He was also conscious of the fact he had chemotherapy scheduled for the next day. The last thing he wanted was to risk putting his stomach on edge.

Fong rode with Uncle to his apartment, and then continued on with Sonny to Fanling. Before Sonny left, Uncle told him he wouldn't be needed for the next few days. When that remark engendered curious looks from both Fong and Sonny, Uncle added, "I have a business meeting locally tomorrow, and then I'm going with a client to Guangzhou the day after. He has his own car and driver."

"Will Ava need me?" Sonny asked.

"Possibly, and if she does you will hear from one of us."

Uncle made his way up the stairs feeling infinitely better than he had the night before. The massage had helped, as had his cautious diet. He entered the apartment to find Lourdes standing over an ironing board in the living room.

"Sir, a Doctor Parker called. He asked that you call his office," she said.

"I'll call him from my bedroom," Uncle said, hiding his annoyance that Parker hadn't called his mobile.

Uncle took off his jacket, sat on the bed, and dialled Parker's office. He was immediately put through to him.

"Mr. Chow, thank you for returning my call. I wanted to remind you that you're scheduled for two more days of treatment starting tomorrow, and I'm wondering how you're feeling?"

"I feel fine — at least, as fine as I can be under the circumstances."

"So you are definitely up for the treatments?"

"Of course."

"Good. That's one of the reasons I was calling. The other is to tell you that, after consulting with Doctor Ma, we have decided to increase your dosage — that is, assuming you have no objections."

"What's behind that decision?"

"Nothing dramatic, it's just that every Monday I like to review my patients' medical charts with Doctor Ma, and she now believes your condition might benefit from a slightly more aggressive treatment. Do you think you can handle that?"

"How can I know until I've had it?"

"Based on your response to your last treatments, Doctor Ma thinks you can," Parker said. "But, as a precaution, why don't you bring an overnight bag with you to the hospital. If your reaction is more severe than we expect, you can stay there for a night or two."

"Is this your recommendation?" Uncle asked.

"It is," Parker said without hesitation.

"Then it would be foolish of me not to follow it," said Uncle.

"Excellent. I'll let her know, and I'll see you sometime during the day."

Uncle put down the phone feeling decidedly uneasy. Had they noticed something in his charts that they hadn't seen before? What wasn't Parker telling him? He would ask, he decided, when they were face to face.

He returned to the living room and eased into his chair. He picked up the racing form with the intention of doing a complete first pass, but soon realized he was too distracted to focus. He might have been able to push aside random thoughts about how Ava was doing, but the added layer of worry that Parker's call had generated was too much. He stood. "I'm going for a walk," he said to Lourdes. "If Ava phones, tell her to call my mobile."

"Can I make you dinner?" Lourdes asked.

"No, not tonight," he said.

When he reached the street, Uncle hesitated before deciding to go to the park. It was relatively quiet there, and he was able to find a bench that wasn't surrounded by exercisers, pedestrians, and prams. He lit a cigarette, took a deep puff, and then stared at it as if it were a stranger. Had smoking ever given him real pleasure, or was it just a stupid addiction? Maybe not pleasure, he thought, but certainly a way to ease stress, and a distraction. He couldn't blame cigarettes for his present condition, because if not them, then what — asbestos, foul air, chemicals in food, old age? His body — anyone's body — had a life span. The time could be preordained, and if it was, why resist?

His phone rang, and he looked at it through three rings as if it were also a stranger, before answering: "*Wei*."

"Uncle, it's Ava, things have heated up."

"How?" he asked, suddenly back in the moment.

"To start with, I'm no longer dealing with Mountie officials in Ottawa, but with the head of the Canadian government's intelligence service in Jakarta."

"So they are moving you up the ladder?"

"I guess you could say that. When I told my contacts in Ottawa about the plane full of cash that could provide them with the thirty million to pay us, they went from being guarded and non-committal to almost enthusiastic. An hour later they phoned me back to say we had a deal in principle, but that I had to speak to a Ryan Poirier—their man in Jakarta. He'll be calling the shots from now on. I've talked to Poirier twice in the last hour. The first time was to review everything I knew about the bank, the Italians, and the plane. When I finished, he said he had to talk to some of his Indonesian military contacts to see if they would come on side. He just called me back with their response."

"Which was?"

"They are prepared to go to Surabaya to intercept the plane, but there is a condition. Initially they were demanding that Cameron be there with them when the plane lands. I told Poirier there was no circumstance under which that was going to happen, and asked if it was a deal-breaker. When he said it was, I offered myself up as an alternative to Cameron."

"What!"

"Uncle, both the Indonesians and the Canadians want assurances that we are prepared to stand behind the information we're giving them, and nothing is better proof of that than being willing to be on the scene when the plane lands," she said. "We can't provide Cameron, so that leaves me."

"Did Poirier accept your offer?"

"Not in so many words. He said he had to talk to the Indonesians, but I believe it will be a go. I mean, why not? I'm the one providing the information."

"I don't like that idea."

"I didn't either at first, but if we want that plane seized, I don't believe we have any other choice," Ava said. "As well, if I'm physically there I will be able to confirm how much money is on the plane."

"That is a good point about the money, but are you saying you don't trust this guy when it comes to that?" Uncle asked.

"I don't know him, but if the Mounties are willing to turn this over to him, then I figure he has to be okay. I mean, if this doesn't work out, they risk losing the information we've promised them."

As much as Uncle was uneasy about Ava going back to Surabaya, he recognized that it did make sense from several viewpoints. Still, he had more questions. "Are we sure the plane is scheduled to land tomorrow night?"

"Not yet, but Poirier told me the Indonesian military has been in touch with the flight control centre director in Surabaya. He has been instructed to let them know the moment a flight plan is registered. They also warned him not to speak a word about this to anyone else," Ava said. "And Uncle, he also confirmed that Brava Italia flights have been arriving every Tuesday for months. That didn't hurt our credibility."

"It is nice they believe us, but what if the director talks? What if he warns the Italians?"

"We have to leave that to the Indonesians to worry about. There's nothing we can do about it," Ava said.

"What happens if you go there and the plane doesn't arrive, or it arrives and isn't carrying a load of cash?"

"I'll be embarrassed, but that's a small price to pay compared to the possible upside. Thirty million dollars is quite a payday."

"Speaking of money, what arrangements have you made with them about how we'll get our share, assuming it arrives?"

"I'd like you to send me the information on the account you set up for Cameron. I'll hold off giving it to them until we know there is actually money to send," said Ava. "I intend to tell them that we won't provide all the information until the money has arrived in the account, but as a sign of good faith I think we should be prepared to forward another batch of transactions as a sort of down payment."

"Yes, I like that. I've seen too many deals like this go under because no one wants to be first to extend trust," he said.

"Well then, if you're satisfied with all of this, it seems we have a plan."

"Except we don't know if the plane is going to arrive tomorrow. When do you need to decide if you're going to Surabaya?"

"I can't wait past tonight or I won't get a flight that will get me there by tomorrow afternoon. So, whether we know the plane's schedule or not, I need to leave Hong Kong tomorrow morning."

"You have to call Poirier before you do. Let's not assume everyone has accepted you as a substitute for Cameron."

"I was going to do that."

"And when you speak to him, run your proposal past him about how we get paid. We don't want that to cause a last-minute problem."

"That was my intention."

"Sorry if I'm being overly concerned, but the last few days have been weighing heavily on me. I could never forgive myself if any harm came to you."

Ava hesitated and then said, "Uncle, I've learned so much from you, including never to make assumptions. So don't worry, I will make sure everyone is in agreement before I get on a plane to Surabaya. Now, I should call Poirier before it gets too late. I'll phone you after I speak to him."

Uncle ended the call. As usual, Ava seemed to have things well in hand, and he knew his worries were more emotional than rational. He began to walk in the direction of his apartment.

When he arrived, he went directly to the kitchen and poured himself a glass of water. He drank it down and poured another. He thought about asking Lourdes for some rice, but then decided there was no point putting something into his body that the chemotherapy might want to expel. Dry heaves weren't pleasant, but they were far superior to actual vomit and a burning esophagus.

Uncle sat in his chair, opened the racing form, and forced himself to focus. He had handicapped the first two races in some detail when his phone rang.

"That didn't take long," he said to Ava. "Was there a problem?"

"None whatsoever. The Indonesians are in agreement with Poirier that my presence in Surabaya will be sufficient, and Poirier agreed to our money-for-information proposal," she said. "The big unknown is still the flight. But like we discussed, I can't wait here until we know, so I'm getting on a flight that's leaving Hong Kong tomorrow morning at ten. Poirier will be meeting me when I land — hopefully with good news."

"Well done."

"I haven't actually accomplished anything yet."

"The first crucial steps have been taken, and the rest will fall into place," he said. "I'll send Sonny to the hotel to pick you up in the morning at eight — if that works for you."

"Sure, that's fine, but won't I be seeing you?"

"Unfortunately, I can't make it," said Uncle. "I have an early meeting concerning some brotherhood business. I'll be out of the apartment for most of the day. In fact, the meeting is about some activities that extend to Guangzhou, so it's possible I might have to go there. But I'll have my mobile with me at all times, and I'll keep it on so you can reach me. I want to be kept updated, so stay in touch."

Ava didn't respond right away, and as Uncle listened to her silence, he knew she didn't believe him entirely but was too polite to question him. That was a relief, because he wasn't sure he could have kept lying if she'd challenged him.

22

UNCLE LEFT HIS APARTMENT AT NINE-FIFTEEN TO WALK to the Queen Elizabeth with his racing form and an overnight bag. Sonny had called him just before he left to tell him that Ava was at the airport and her flight to Surabaya was on time. It was going to be a day full of worry until he knew the Brava Italia flight had landed, had on board its normal amount of cash, and had been seized by the Indonesians. In a perverse way, the chemotherapy would be a welcome distraction.

The street was busy as it always was at that time of the morning, but Uncle had given himself ample time to get to the hospital, even walking slowly. At about the halfway point, he stopped at a stand to buy his newspapers, and noticed out of the corner of his eye a woman in a bright pink blouse and jeans coming to a stop several paces behind him. He looked at her, but she averted her eyes, turned, and walked to the window of a women's clothing shop. When Uncle left the stand, she was still there looking inside. He didn't think much of it until five minutes later, when he was stopped at a red light. As he waited for it to change, he casually glanced around and caught a flash of the pink blouse. It was the same woman, and she was beginning to look vaguely familiar.

He continued his walk to the Queen Elizabeth, increasingly conscious that the woman in pink was keeping him in sight. *It probably means nothing*, he thought, *and she certainly isn't any kind of threat.* But as pedestrian traffic thinned and he neared the hospital, her presence was starting to annoy him. When he reached R Block, he came to a halt. If she was tailing him, he didn't want her to know where he was going. But on the other hand, he had his appointment. Uncle shook his head in frustration, and then started up the steps that led to the entrance. He went inside and headed directly towards the outpatient clinic. Just before he went through the doors, he stopped and looked back. The woman was in the lobby. He stared at her, and she looked uncomfortable. In that instant he recognized her — it was Sonny's girlfriend.

He got her to follow me, Uncle thought angrily. Now that she had, there was nothing he could do except make sure it didn't happen again. But what could she report to Sonny? She had seen him go into the hospital with an overnight bag, but of course wouldn't know why. Still, Sonny obviously suspected something was going on with Uncle or he wouldn't have asked her to do it. And then there were all the questions he — and Ava — had been asking. Uncle would talk to Sonny, he decided, and tell him to back off.

Within a few hours, thoughts about Sonny and his girlfriend were the furthest thing from his mind. What Parker had described as a "slightly more aggressive" treatment turned his head to mush. His body didn't react well to it either, but thankfully the nausea wasn't as violent as it had been during his first treatment. What was worse, though, was how drained of energy he felt. When the IV was removed after the morning round, he stood to go to the bathroom and felt his legs give way. He managed to grab the arm of the chair and stay upright. A nurse offered to help him, but he told her he just needed to gather himself and that he'd be okay. It took several minutes before that was even partially true, and then he wobbled his way to the bathroom.

Doctor Ma came to see him before the second round.

"I heard you had some difficulty earlier," she said.

"I don't seem to have much strength."

"It will return, but are you up to this afternoon's treatment?"

"I'm here, so we might as well do it," he said.

"Let me know if it becomes too much for you to handle," she said.

With the IV back in place, Uncle settled into the chair, and was trying for the third or fourth time to focus on the Happy Valley races when his phone rang. He saw Ava's name.

"Have you arrived safely?" he asked.

"I have, and I was met by Ryan Poirier."

"How was he?"

"Suspicious. He asked me to produce my Jennie Kwong passport, which I did," she said. "Thankfully I booked the flight in that name, because I wouldn't have put it past him to check the passenger list."

"You shouldn't be surprised at his attitude given how strange all of this must seem to him."

"I wasn't surprised, and I wasn't offended. In fact, our conversation ended on a high note," she said. "The Indonesians have confirmed that the Brava Italia flight is scheduled to arrive today, and Poirier told me that an elite specialized combat unit is getting ready now to stake out positions at the airport. The Italians are going to be in for quite a shock."

"Now let's just hope that the plane is carrying the usual amount of money."

"I'll know shortly after it lands. Poirier and I won't be part of the active seizure operation, but he tells me we'll be going to the airport with the troops, and we'll be close enough to watch the action and be among the first people to get on the plane."

"I am so glad you won't be directly involved."

"I have no idea how it will play out, but I can't imagine that the Italians will offer much resistance against an entire military unit."

"They are unpredictable, so I wouldn't be surprised by anything they do," said Uncle.

"Well, whatever happens, I'll call you as soon as it's over."

"I'll be waiting," he said.

He turned his attention back to Happy Valley, and then felt his eyes become heavy. He closed them for what he thought was a few seconds, but when he opened them, he saw Parker looking down at him.

"You have slept away a good part of the afternoon," Parker said. "Doctor Ma told me the treatment has affected your strength."

"I feel tired and a bit weak, that's all. I'm sure once you take the IV out and I move around a bit, I'll improve."

"That may be the case, but I really think you should spend the night here so we can monitor your situation. I see you brought a bag with you, so we can make arrangements now."

"Is that really necessary?" Uncle asked.

"No, but it would be wise. And I prefer to err on the side of caution when it comes to my patients," said Parker. "We'll see how you are in the morning before making a decision to continue with another day of treatment tomorrow. I still think we need to be aggressive, but I don't want to overdo it."

"Can I get a private room?" Uncle asked, and when he saw Parker frown he added, "I'll pay for it of course. It is just that I'm in the middle of some complicated business negotiations, and I need my privacy."

"And if I can't make that arrangement?"

"Then I'd rather go home."

"I'll see what I can do," said Parker.

Spending a night in the hospital was something Uncle did not want to do, but he respected Parker's judgement and thought it would be foolish not to listen to him. And he had already spun his story about going to Guangzhou with a friend to Ava and Sonny, so if he wasn't at the apartment his excuse was in place. Besides, nothing could be worse than going to the apartment and becoming ill enough that he had to be taken to hospital. There was no way he could cover that up.

Then Sonny's girlfriend came to mind. What had she told Sonny? Whatever it was, Uncle thought, he couldn't imagine Sonny ever confronting him. He wouldn't raise the subject of the girlfriend following him, he now decided. It was better to pretend he'd never seen her, and carry on as usual.

The chairs around Uncle gradually lost their patients until he was the last one left. He started to think that Parker was having a problem, and that maybe his options would be to share a room with another patient or go home to the apartment. If it came to that, he decided, he'd go home. Ava was going to be calling, and depending on how things went, he didn't want to have to be careful with his words.

As he began to steel himself for a trip home, Parker came into the room with Doctor Ma.

"You are a lucky man," said Parker. "We managed to get you a private room. Doctor Ma is going to be on duty tonight and will be able to check on you."

"I appreciate both of those things very much," said Uncle, starting to rise from the chair.

"No, don't do that," Ma said. "We'll get you a wheelchair, and an orderly will take you to your room. When you're settled, I will come and see you."

"You are in good hands," said Parker. "I'll see you in the morning and we'll make a decision about continuing treatment then. One benefit of the private room is that if we decide to proceed, we can do it there, so you won't have to leave your bed."

Ten minutes later, Uncle was wheeled into a private room on the seventh floor. After he put on a hospital gown and climbed into bed, a nurse appeared at the door carrying a large bottle of water and a glass.

"You need to keep hydrated. It is important that you drink as much water as you can handle," she said.

"What about food?"

"Someone will bring you dinner shortly. It will be something bland, I'm afraid. Eat what you can."

Uncle nodded, and then his phone rang. It sat on top of his suit jacket, which he had left on a chair. The nurse picked up the phone and handed it to him. He saw Ava's name again.

"I have to take this, and it is a rather private call... *Wei*, Ava," he said as the nurse left.

"The worst is over. The plane landed full of money and we secured it," she said. "But, Uncle, I've never been involved in something quite so awful."

"What happened?" Uncle asked.

"When the plane landed, it went into a hangar and was quickly joined by a van containing the two local Italians," she said. "As soon as the hangar door closed, the army unit surrounded it, and then a moment later they burst in through the front door. I was close enough to hear the first shot coming from inside, and then all hell broke loose."

"The Italians?"

"Both dead, along with the pilot."

"So they resisted?"

"I don't know if you can call one shot resistance, but the Indonesians used that as an excuse. I've never seen so much blood. The hangar looked like an abattoir."

Uncle hesitated. "No matter how it was handled, it is better that they are dead."

"Poirier doesn't think so. He wanted them taken alive. The Indonesians obviously did not."

"Did he react badly?"

"He showed his displeasure to the Indonesians in a subtle way. Otherwise he was very professional."

"It shouldn't come as a surprise to him that someone in authority in Jakarta wouldn't want the Italians to be interrogated," Uncle said.

"I don't think he was surprised, just disappointed," she said. "He does know the game."

"As do we."

"Yes — as do we, Uncle," Ava said.

"So what happens now?"

"They're removing the bodies and the van. When that's done, I'll count the money, take some pictures, get as many official signatures as I can, and catch an early flight out of here tomorrow morning."

"I am glad you made the decision to go."

"Me too."

"There is always a risk when you are dealing with so many moving parts, but if you had not gone it would have been very difficult for us to put the Italians behind us. Now we know for certain those that were in Indonesia won't be pursuing us."

"And we have the money."

"Getting the money is all well and good, but it was the Italians who were weighing on me."

"I know, Uncle."

"Will the Indonesians hold onto the money for now?"

"Yes, but they have their agreement with the Canadians; the Canadians have their deal with us; and we have the information that everyone is waiting for."

"It will be a few days then, before it arrives in our Kowloon bank?"

"I would hope it is no longer than that," Ava said. "Now, I should get going. I have money to count."

"Call me in the morning when everything is settled and you know which flight you are on," Uncle said. "If for some reason you can't reach me, talk to Sonny. He will meet you at the airport."

Ava hesitated, and Uncle wondered if she was going to ask him why he might be out of reach. Instead, she simply said, "See you tomorrow."

23

AFTER SPEAKING TO AVA, UNCLE FELT SEVERAL DAYS
of accumulated stress begin to drain from his body. The
Italians were dead. Ava, Perkasa, and the others were safe.
The money had been secured. His mind could stop racing.

A nurse entered his room carrying a dinner tray, but he
told her he wasn't hungry and asked her to turn off the lights.
He lay in the dark and thought about how fate had once
again treated him and Ava kindly. But had it been for the last
time? Would there ever be another job for them as a team?
The idea that this might be their last filled him with panic,
until he remembered that it didn't really matter: he and Ava
would always be close.

Uncle closed his eyes, and the darkness took on a different dimension. Like the previous day, when he'd felt isolated
from his physical surroundings, his mind now seemed disconnected from the body that was failing him. He accepted
the need for chemotherapy, but he doubted it would make
much difference. Parker had talked about buying time. The
question was whether the price was worth it. As long as his
mind remained sharp, he thought he could handle whatever

pain the cancer imposed. It couldn't be much worse than his reaction to chemo, could it? Without chemo, how long could he last — six months? With the chemo, how many months could he add, and what would their quality be? Since he was already in the hospital, Uncle decided he would endure another day of treatment, but then he would talk to Parker about discontinuing the chemotherapy.

Uncle's phone rang. *Has something unexpected happened in Surabaya?* he thought.

"Uncle, this is Sonny."

The unease vanished, to be replaced with irritation. "Yes, Sonny, what do you want?"

"I was just wondering if you're going to need me tonight or tomorrow."

There was a nuance in Sonny's voice that wasn't typical. *The girlfriend told him I came to the hospital,* Uncle thought. "No, I don't. I'm in Guangzhou and I'm not sure when I'm getting back," he said. "But Ava will be flying into Hong Kong from Surabaya tomorrow, and I'd like you to meet her at the airport."

"Did it go well there?"

"Very well. In fact it couldn't have gone much better," he said. "I'll tell Ava to call you when her schedule is set."

He hung up and lay flat on his back. He started to think about the day ahead, but before it took shape, he fell into a dream.

Uncle seldom dreamt these days, but when he did Gui-San was usually his focus. This time, Ava, his mother, and his sister were with her. All the women in his life sitting together on a sunlit beach, chatting and looking at an expanse of water shaped like Shenzhen Bay, except the water was a bright blue, unlike the dark murk that filled Shenzhen.

He approached the women feeling a little self-conscious. They were smiling and seemed completely at ease with one another, and Uncle wondered if they would object to him intruding. His mother noticed him first, and her smile turned into a broad grin. "Come and sit with us," she said.

The women, sitting side by side, moved to create a space for him between Gui-San and Ava. Uncle lowered himself onto the sand.

"We were just telling Ava that we can hardly wait for you to join us," Gui-San said as she tucked her arm through his.

"Yes, it is so peaceful here," his sister said. "There is nothing to cause worry or regrets about what you leave behind."

"I missed you, of course," Gui-San said, squeezing his arm, "but I knew you would be with me eventually. I've been patient, and time here passes quickly."

Uncle tried to speak, but to his distress he couldn't force the words from his mouth. Instead he turned his head to look at Ava.

"You seem surprised to see me here, but there's no reason to be," she said. "Gui-San invited me to pay her a visit, and I've always wanted to meet your family."

"But how?" he finally managed to say.

"You will learn the answer to that question in good time," Gui-San said.

Uncle woke with a start, his body cold and clammy. Was that a reaction to the dream, or a lingering side effect of the chemotherapy? And what about the dream itself? Had it been chemically induced? What did Ava's presence signify? Had something happened in Surabaya?

He slipped out of bed, steadied himself, and walked to the

bathroom. When he returned he checked the time and saw it was already past seven. He had slept through the night. He climbed back into the bed, and almost on cue the door opened and a nurse appeared.

"I checked on you during the night," she said. "You seemed to be sleeping soundly. Did you have a good night?"

"I did."

"Good. Someone will be by shortly with something light to eat, and Doctor Parker will be here around ten to start your next treatment."

When the nurse left, Uncle reached for his phone, and saw there had been no missed calls during the night. If Ava hadn't been in his dream, he wouldn't have thought twice about it, but now he felt a touch of anxiety. He thought she should have been at least on her way to the airport in Surabaya by now, and considered calling her. Before that idea took root, his phone rang.

"Ava, where are you?" he answered.

"I've just arrived at the airport."

"How did it end last night?"

"There was about seventy million U.S. on the plane. The Canadians are ready to send us thirty million as soon as tomorrow," she said. "I have already provided Poirier with the Kowloon banking information. He was slightly surprised, but quite pleased to see Andy Cameron's name attached to the account. It bolstered the credibility of our story."

"That is fantastic news. Good work, my girl."

"Thanks, Uncle, but it wasn't just good work on my part. We are a team."

"Yes, we are," he said, trying to dampen his emotions. "When does your flight leave?"

"In half an hour. I'll be in Hong Kong in time for lunch. Will you be meeting me at the airport?"

"I can't. I'm still with my friend in Guangzhou, but Sonny is expecting you to call him with your flight information. He'll pick you up."

"I'm surprised he didn't drive you to Guangzhou," she said.

"My friend has his own driver."

"That must have upset Sonny. He's quite possessive when it comes to driving you."

"Since when do I need Sonny's approval for anything?"

"I meant no offence, Uncle. We just worry about you."

"There is no reason for that either."

"I know, but you can't fault us for caring."

Uncle thought he detected an insinuation in that comment, and quickly changed the subject. "I have to go. My friend is waiting for me. We have plans for the day, and now thanks to you I can enjoy them with a clear head and a peaceful heart. Have a safe flight. I'll see you tomorrow or the day after," he said, and then hung up.

I handled that badly, he thought.

24

THE MORNING PASSED SLOWLY. PARKER'S STRENGTH-
ened concoction knocked him for a loop. Uncle threw up
the plain white bread he'd had for breakfast, and felt so weak
after that he needed help getting to the bathroom. Parker
visited him at eleven and was so alarmed at his condition
that he stopped the treatment.

"I apologize profusely," Parker said. "It appears I've misjudged what you can handle."

"And I may have misjudged what I'm actually prepared
to endure," said Uncle.

"What are you saying?"

"I've been thinking about all of this for the last few days,"
Uncle said. "Is there really a point to it?"

"A point?" asked Parker, his expression suggesting he
already knew the answer.

"The cancer can't be cured, can it?"

Parker shook his head. "No, Mr. Chow, but it can be
slowed."

"When we talked in your office, you were vague about how
much time the chemotherapy might buy me, but I remember

you spoke of months, not years. Is that accurate?"

"Yes, but I also said that every patient reacts differently. There is no way of predicting accurately how much time can be added by treatment."

Uncle closed his eyes and licked his dry lips. "I have such a thirst. Could you pour me a glass of water, doctor?"

Parker half filled a glass, and then helped Uncle sit up so he could drink. When he finished, Uncle lay down again and stared up at the doctor. "I am not afraid to die," he said. "I have been in several situations where death was a possibility and I felt no fear. In fact, on at least one occasion I was more than prepared to accept it."

"Not many people have that attitude. You are a fortunate man."

"I have certainly been fortunate when it comes to the people in my life," said Uncle. "I worry about them more than myself. It may sound egotistical to say my death will leave a hole in their lives, but I know it will."

"Are your affairs in order?" Parker asked.

"More or less."

"I don't wish to suggest there is a great urgency, but I have found it helps many patients to prepare for the inevitable. It brings them closure."

"I will take your advice," said Uncle.

"Have you decided to stop taking chemotherapy?" asked Parker.

"I think I have, unless you can give me a compelling reason why I should continue."

Parker shook his head. "I'm sorry, Mr. Chow."

"Then that's that," said Uncle. "I will take my chances without the treatment."

"I'll cancel what was planned, but I still want you to stay here for the day so I can monitor you. I want to feel certain you're strong enough to manage on your own."

"Believe me, I don't feel up to going anywhere right now," Uncle said with a wan smile.

"And you will still be my patient. I'll expect to see you every few weeks, and I'll be available whenever you need me."

"That is very considerate."

Parker nodded and started to leave the room, then stopped and turned back towards Uncle. "Your family doctor, Doctor Cho, told me a little about you. He said you were a remarkable man. I now have a better understanding of what he meant."

Shortly after Parker left, Uncle drifted off to sleep. He was awakened by the nurse's voice saying, "He's all yours." Uncle opened his eyes, and to his shock saw Ava standing at the foot of his bed. He watched her walk to a chair in the corner of the room. She carried it next to the bed and sat, putting her hand on top of his. She then lowered her head onto the bed, and with her eyes tightly shut, began to whisper what he thought was a prayer that invoked the name of St. Jude.

"I couldn't bear the thought of you being here alone," she said, looking at him through eyes brimming with tears.

"I had a feeling you didn't believe my story about going to Guangzhou," he said.

"I wanted to, but other thoughts, other facts, kept intruding."

"We know each other too well," he said.

"Is that a bad thing?"

"No, my dear. Was it Sonny who told you I was here?"

"Yes."

"He had that girlfriend of his follow me. He probably thinks I did not notice."

"He's just worried about you, Uncle. We all are."

"Who is 'we'?"

"Sonny, me, and Lourdes."

"Anyone else?"

"No."

"I want to keep it that way, at least for now."

"Yes, Uncle," Ava said.

"Did they tell you what is wrong with me?" Uncle said, indicating the nurse's station outside.

Ava stroked the back of his hand. "Only that you've been taking chemotherapy, but I know you've been complaining about stomach problems for some time, and when you threw up blood on the street a few days ago . . . well, I assumed the worst."

"It started a while ago, and fool that I am, I ignored it for many months. But then I could not let it go on anymore."

"Stomach cancer?"

"Yes."

"What caused it?"

"Smoking, they think."

"But you're still smoking."

"My family doctor, Cho, referred me to a *gweilo* specialist named Parker. I asked him if I should stop. He told me cigarettes couldn't cause much more damage than they'd already done, and that withdrawal would only give me stress," Uncle said. "I quite like Parker. He's honest and pragmatic, a good combination."

"But they're treating the cancer, aren't they?"

"There is not much they can do," he said, trying to convey calm. "They cannot perform surgery, and even if they could, at my age it would likely kill me. Parker prescribed chemotherapy to buy me some time, but I've had enough of it. I don't need time that badly."

"Is there a different treatment available somewhere else, like in the United States or Switzerland?"

Uncle placed his free hand on top of hers and squeezed. "Ava, I am over eighty years old. Why would I want to become a desperate man now, when I have spent my entire adult life being in control? I've made up my mind and I am going to see things through my way. I value my dignity, and I have a reputation that I intend to uphold. So, Ava, I am telling you, as much as I respect you, do not try to change my mind, and please keep the rest of the world at bay. I understand about Sonny and Lourdes, and I know they would never dare to talk about me to anyone else. You are not quite so afraid of me."

"Amanda gets married in January," she said softly.

"And?"

"She needs me here. So I'll be staying in Hong Kong until at least then."

"I am sure she will appreciate that."

"When I'm not helping out with the wedding, I can spend time with you. I'll visit every day. We can meet in the mornings for jook."

"I do not intend to live on congee alone," he said, a tiny smile playing on his lips.

"You know what I mean."

"I think I do," he said, gazing at her.

"We'll make the best of the time that is left together, and

hopefully that's longer than any of these doctors anticipates," she said.

"I like your optimism, but there are some things I need to discuss with you," Uncle said. "If we do it now, then we never need discuss these things again."

"Do we have to, Uncle?"

"It would give me some peace. I have been thinking about these things for some time now."

"Yes, Uncle."

"You know that I have no family here. And I have been in Hong Kong for so many years that my ties to Wuhan are more wishful thinking than real."

Ava nodded.

"I met with a lawyer after I first suspected there was something wrong with me, and told him to draft a will. When I get out of here I intend to finalize it. You will be named as my executor."

"Uncle, I do not want to talk about your will," Ava said.

"Perhaps not, but I do. And then, as I said, it will be done, and it will be one less thing for me to worry about."

"Uncle, please," Ava said, almost mournfully.

He hesitated, but resolved to continue, knowing there might never be a better time. "I am going to leave ten million HK to Lourdes, and I am giving her the apartment. If she wants to sell it and move back to the Philippines and live like a millionaire, she can do that. I am also leaving ten million to Uncle Fong. He did not save enough for his retirement, and he has no children to care for him. Ava, I need you to look in on him from time to time. He has been a good friend to me."

"Yes, he has been a good friend," Ava said, and to his satisfaction she seemed willing to listen to him now.

"Sonny is a different matter," Uncle said hesitantly. "I am leaving him the car and some money, but we need to do more than that for him."

"Like what?"

"You must hire him as your driver."

"Uncle, I have no need —"

"Listen to me, Ava. Sonny is not a man to be left to his own devices. He needs structure; he needs to feel he belongs to something. If he is on his own, he will get into trouble, and the kind of trouble Sonny would get into would earn him more than a slap on the wrist. Ava, no one could be more loyal."

"I know that, but how could it work? I live in Toronto, not in Hong Kong."

"Things could change when I'm gone, especially if you go into business with May Ling."

"Yes, Uncle, but that is beside the point. I have no plans to live in Hong Kong, so I don't know what you expect me to do about Sonny."

"Anything will do. Tell him he is working for you, but when you aren't in Hong Kong you want him to drive for your father or Amanda Yee. Come up with something, anything. We need to keep Sonny occupied."

"All right," Ava said with resignation.

"You need to think about a future without me," Uncle said, squeezing her hand again.

Ava lowered her head. "I don't like talking this way."

"You need to talk to Parker. He brings clarity to things," Uncle said. "When I asked him what I should do about my condition, he told me I should get my affairs in order. I appreciated his honesty and I am taking his advice. You are going to inherit the bulk of my estate. What you do with it is up to you. All I ask is that you look after Uncle Fong and keep Sonny out of trouble."

He watched Ava wipe her eyes and wished there had been another way to do this.

"Uncle, I don't want any of this to happen," she said.

"Neither do I, but here we are."

"Ms. Lee," a voice said from the doorway.

Uncle looked up to see a nurse standing nearby. She seemed angry, and he couldn't understand why.

"We agreed to a five-minute visit with your grandfather. These are not our usual visitation hours," she said to Ava. "You need to leave now."

"I'm sorry, I lost track of time," Ava said, standing.

Uncle looked up at her. "I am glad things are settled. I was worried about how I was going to tell you. You have made it easier for me."

"I'll be back tonight," she said.

"At regular visiting hours," the nurse added.

"At five-thirty," Ava said to Uncle.

"I'll be leaving here tomorrow," he said.

"And I'll be here to get you."

"Ms. Lee," the nurse said.

Ava bent over and kissed Uncle on the forehead. "I love you," she whispered.

He watched her walk towards the door and felt a surge of emotion he hadn't experienced since he'd lost Gui-San.

"Ava, I love you too," he whispered.

She turned back to him. "Yes, Uncle, what did you say?"

"Nothing, my girl. Nothing at all."

PART TWO

(1)
Kowloon, Hong Kong
January 2016

SINCE ABANDONING HIS CHEMOTHERAPY TREATMENTS
in September, Uncle had been careful not to fall back into
his old routines. During the week, he ate congee most mornings with Ava, and a lot of white rice and other bland foods
prepared by Lourdes for dinner. He had cut back on his
cigarette consumption considerably, and most days managed to forego his beloved San Miguel beer. His weekends,
though, were another story.

In October, Uncle had confided the details of his condition to his old friend Fong, and since then the pair had
begun meeting regularly for dinner on Saturday nights. These
weekly dinners were the one time in the week that Uncle
risked upsetting his stomach. He would have a few beers,
smoke some cigarettes, and eat food that had more flavour
and texture but still wasn't overly spicy. Uncle and Fong took
turns choosing the restaurant for their Saturday night dinner, and this week Fong had selected a hot pot restaurant in
Hong Kong's Central District that they both liked. Uncle was

known to the owner, and he and Fong were quickly seated when they arrived. Within minutes of sitting down, two cold beers were on the table in front of them, and a flame was lit under the pot containing the chicken broth. Fong ordered platters of shrimp, beef, squid, mushrooms, and tofu, and when the server left, he raised his beer bottle to Uncle. "Here's to a fine meal, and may we have many more," he said.

"Indeed," said Uncle as he sipped carefully.

"When I spoke with Lourdes earlier today, I asked about Ava. She told me she hadn't been around very much this week," said Fong, putting down his bottle after a healthy swig. "That's unusual, isn't it? I thought you saw her every day."

"Her half-brother Michael is marrying Amanda Yee today. Ava is the maid of honour. She's been tied up all week with the preparations."

"Am I remembering correctly that Amanda is one of Ava's new business partners?"

"She owns a small part of the business. Ava and May Ling Wong gave it to her rather than making her invest, since Amanda is the one who'll be running things on a day-to-day basis. May Ling is still strongly involved, of course, but she and her husband live in Wuhan," he said, and then paused before adding: "And while Ava has been spending a lot of time with me lately, when I'm no longer here, she'll return to Toronto."

Fong flicked a hand in the air as if to swipe away Uncle's last remark. "With Amanda marrying Michael, that is adding more complications to Ava's already complicated family life," he said.

"Her rather prominent role in the wedding isn't going to

make things any easier either," said Uncle. "She'll be meeting her other half-brothers for the first time, and I imagine she'll run into Elizabeth Lee."

"Her father's first wife?"

"Yes, and the one he still lives with. Marcus sent Ava's mother to Canada decades ago. Mind you, he looked after her very well, along with Ava and her older sister, so I give him credit for that."

"Is Ava close to him?"

"I don't know how strong the emotional attachment is," Uncle said. "I do know that when the brother, Michael, ran into trouble last year, Ava came to his rescue at her father's request, so there is at least a sense of family obligation."

"I hope the wedding goes well," Fong said. "I hate the thought of Ava being disrespected. You know how awful first wives and their families can be to kids from a second or third marriage."

"I hardly slept last night worrying about it," Uncle said with a wan smile. "I know she's strong, but I can't help feeling protective."

"You made...you *are* a great team," Fong said, correcting himself. "When you retired as Mountain Master, many of us were concerned about how you would fill your days. None of us expected that you and Ava would accomplish the things you did."

"We did a lot of good, didn't we?"

"And you made a lot of money."

"That's true, but it was never about the money. Not really. At the start it was about helping friends in need, and then after Ava joined forces with me, the jobs we took on were really just my way of keeping her close."

"You were always more than just partners."

"It's true. And it began almost from the moment I first spoke to her. I hadn't met her in person yet, so it was on the phone. She was in Shenzhen chasing down the same thief that Andy and Carlo were after. She had already impressed them with her fighting ability, but now she was haranguing them about the money. She felt they had settled for too little and wanted to go after more. I was brought in to make a decision. I remember the conversation like it was yesterday. Ava was polite, respectful, and stated her case in such an intelligent and logical way that I gave in to her without argument. She ended up finding more than twice the money the boys had agreed to take."

"When did you actually meet her face to face?"

"The next day, after I arranged for her to be released from jail in Shenzhen."

"I don't know that story."

Uncle smiled. "She and Andy were attacked by the thief's bodyguards outside his office. Ava put them both on the ground, but it turned out they were off-duty cops, and she was arrested. I had to call in a few favours to get her out of that jam. Later that night we met for dinner, and my earlier impressions of her were strengthened to the point that I offered her a job before dinner had even ended. She said no."

"She did? What changed her mind?"

"The next day I offered her a full partnership, and when she still hesitated, I asked her to take on one job with me as a trial run. She accepted and we never discussed our business relationship again. We simply moved on to a second job and kept on going for another ten years."

Their food arrived, and talk dwindled as portions of shrimp, mushrooms, beef, and more were put into the broth to cook. When they bobbed to the surface they were deemed ready to eat, and were plucked from the pot in small mesh baskets, then dipped in a variety of sauces. Fong had made a sauce laden with chili peppers for himself, while Uncle mixed light soy and oyster sauce together for his.

"Do you want more?" Fong asked when the beef and shrimp platters were depleted.

"I'd better not, but I'll have another beer," said Uncle.

When two more beers arrived, Fong put down his chopsticks and asked, "Are you still planning to go to Shanghai?"

"Yes, I intend to go sometime in the next week or two. It has been nearly six months since I was there."

"Does Xu know about your . . . condition?" asked Fong.

"No."

"I've never met him," said Fong, deciding not to follow up on his question. "Is he anything like his father?"

Xu's father — also named Xu — had been part of the Fanling triads with Fong and Uncle. The three men had been close friends, but when Xu the elder moved to Shanghai to start his own gang, Fong had lost touch with him. Uncle, however, visited him often. During those visits he had also established a strong relationship with the younger Xu, and when the young man had decided to follow in his father's footsteps, Uncle had mentored him, and had even sponsored him when he took the Thirty-Six Oaths. When Xu the elder died, his son became the gang's Mountain Master, and Uncle had adopted a role as his senior advisor.

"Yes, in some ways. Like his father, Xu is clever, hardworking, considerate to those who work for him, and he generates great loyalty and respect," Uncle said. "But he has more ambition than his father, and can be colder, more calculating. That isn't to say he's sly, because he's not; he's actually very straightforward. But he isn't a man to shy away from challenges, and he has surrounded himself with talented people who would do anything for him. I don't believe there is a gang in Hong Kong who could defeat Shanghai in a turf war."

"Does Xu have any ambitions in Hong Kong?"

"Only as a market for the high-end knock-off goods produced by his factories," Uncle said, and then hesitated before deciding he could be completely open with Fong. "Strictly between us, I am trying to convince him to run for the position of chairman of the triad societies. He believes in the extended brotherhood, he has vision, and he understands that fostering co-operation between the gangs is the best way to build a strong collective future."

"All things you believed in," said Fong.

"Yes, and for good reason."

"I'm not suggesting otherwise, but you know there are Mountain Masters who prefer to do things their own way. Not all of them accept your idea of co-operation or your vision for a strong collective future," said Fong. "I've also heard that Li in Guangzhou wants the chairmanship."

"He wants it so he can render it useless."

"Maybe, but he's smart and tough, and he has the support of many other gangs."

"Well, the election is months away, so it is a bit soon to start speculating about who will run and what kind of support they can generate."

"Is Xu leaning towards running?"

"I think so."

"Then good luck in getting him to commit," said Fong.

Uncle lit a cigarette and felt immediately queasy. He put the cigarette out and sipped his beer to get rid of the taste in his mouth. "Thank you, but convincing Xu to run for chairman isn't the only reason I'm going to Shanghai," he said. "I need to tell Xu that I'm ill, and I have decided that now is the time to introduce Xu to Ava."

"They've never met?"

"I've never even mentioned her to him, or vice versa."

"Why not?"

Uncle shrugged. "As you know, I have always endeavoured to keep certain parts of my life separate. There were things that I never felt the need to share. For example, until I took you to the Ancestor Worship Hall in Yuen Long, no one else knew about the niche."

"And even after you left the gang, you never shared the name of your contact in the Hong Kong police department."

"Tian knew, but he was the one who brought us together," Uncle said, referring to the man who had been his triad mentor. "Tian was as tight-lipped and secretive as me."

"But why would you keep Ava and Xu secret from each other?"

"They exist in different spheres. The only thing they have in common is me."

"So why introduce them now?" asked Fong.

"Because I'm not going to be here forever, and I'm counting on them to support each other after I'm gone," he said. "Maybe it's an old man's ego speaking, but Ava and I would never have been as successful as we were if, from time to time, I hadn't tapped into my network of friends and brothers. And

I like to think that my counsel has helped Xu become the Mountain Master and the man he is today."

"So you want Ava to be able to use Xu's connections, and you want him to use her as an advisor?" Fong said, sounding doubtful.

"Why not?" Uncle said briskly. "I don't know what Ava will do when I'm gone, but if she decides to run a business with May Ling and Amanda in Asia, having strong triad connections would certainly be advantageous. As for Ava advising Xu, I've never met anyone in the brotherhood or elsewhere who thinks things through as thoroughly as she does. She could be an objective sounding board for him."

"I do see the logic in that," Fong admitted.

"And there's something else. One of the challenges Xu is facing in Shanghai is what to do with all the money he's generating. If he had a way to quietly, maybe even secretly, invest in legitimate businesses, it would be of tremendous help to him in the long term. Ava and May Ling are in the early days of their business together. I know they've each put in one hundred million U.S. dollars, but an infusion of another two or three hundred million with no strings attached could change the type and size of businesses they can invest in."

"May Ling would have to be told about Xu, no?" asked Fong.

"May is pragmatic, and if Xu can convince Ava to take his money, then I'm sure Ava could bring May on side."

Fong nodded and then furrowed his brow. "You seem quite pale, Uncle. Are you feeling okay?"

"I'm not used to speaking this much. It seems to have tired me," he said. "I also shouldn't have tried to smoke, or maybe it's just that the food and beer are catching up to me."

"Do you want to go home?"

"I think I should."

Fong paid their bill, gripped Uncle gently by the arm, and walked him through the restaurant. Sonny was outside, standing by the Mercedes. As soon he saw them emerge from the restaurant, he rushed over to them.

"He's not feeling terrific," Fong said. "You should take him directly to the apartment. I'll catch a taxi back to Fanling."

"Sorry to fade like this," Uncle said. "It was a fine evening until a few minutes ago."

"It was a fine evening...period. And we'll have many more of them," said Fong.

Sonny helped Uncle get into the back seat and pointed the car in the direction of Kowloon. Uncle leaned back against the headrest and closed his eyes. He opened them a few times to check the car's progress. Every time he did, he saw Sonny glancing worriedly at him in the rear-view mirror.

When they reached the apartment building, Sonny insisted on walking up the stairs with Uncle, and for once there were no objections. Sonny held his arm more tightly than Fong had, which allowed him to steady and at times almost carry Uncle as they made their way up to the apartment. As soon as they entered, Uncle went directly to his bedroom. As he lay down he heard Sonny whispering to Lourdes.

Uncle fell asleep in his clothes. He was wakened by an overwhelming bout of nausea that made him dizzy. He struggled to get out of bed, and then stumbled from the room and lurched towards the bathroom. He opened the door, but before he could get to the toilet his stomach heaved and much of that evening's dinner was spewed onto the floor. He reached for the towel rod to keep himself steady, then his knees buckled. The last thing Uncle saw before passing out on the floor was blood mixed with his vomit. There seemed to be a pool of it.

2

THE NEXT FEW HOURS WERE A BLUR. UNCLE HAD A vague recollection of being carried down the stairs on a cot by paramedics; of arriving at the Queen Elizabeth Hospital in an ambulance; of being taken to a room and given an IV in his arm; and of Doctor Parker hovering at the end of his bed.

At one point, Uncle was alert enough to say to Parker, "I think I overdid it."

"You have to stop eating and drinking the way you did tonight," Parker said. "If you keep it up, you will not only shorten what time you have left, you will also be in significantly more pain."

Uncle wanted to nod but didn't have the strength. He fell asleep.

The next thing he was conscious of was a sweet aroma tickling his nose. He forced his eyes open and saw Ava's familiar profile. Her head was resting on the bed and one of her hands lay on top of his. He gently pried her hand free, placed his on her head, and began gently stroking her hair. She looked up at him with tears welling in her eyes.

"No crying," he said.

She lowered her head, Uncle's hand still resting on it, as light as air. "Doctor Parker says you're going to be okay. He thinks you might be able to go home tomorrow," she said.

"I am pleased to hear that, although I'm not sure how many more times I will."

"That depends on how well you look after yourself."

"I do not put much value in buying a day here and there."

"Please, don't talk like that, Uncle," she said.

He heard pain in her voice and knew he shouldn't have been so casual. "Ava, I have been so lucky in my life. I never thought I would live to this age, and I never thought I would die in my own bed," he said. "There were times..." he began, and then paused to find the right words.

Ava lifted her head, her attention completely focused on him.

"The worst time was when we swam from China," he said, realizing this was finally the time to tell her about Gui-San.

"You've never told me that story."

"It still causes me grief to think about it," he said. "We were starving in Wuhan — that goddamn Great Leap Forward — but I was young, and with some other young people, I decided to leave for Hong Kong. We made it to Shenzhen Bay, gathered what strength we had left, and got into the water to swim to Hong Kong.

"There were twelve of us, and we had a wooden door that we used as a raft. We took turns on the raft, the others swimming alongside or clinging to it and pushing it along. We swam all night. The water was dark, filthy, and cold. I have never been so frightened — and not just for myself. The woman I loved and was planning to marry was one of the twelve," he said, and then stopped.

Ava gripped his hand. "You have never mentioned a woman, Uncle."

He nodded. "I know, because I couldn't bring myself to discuss her with you or anyone else," he said. "Uncle Fong, Xu, and a few other brothers knew she had been with me on the swim, but even with them I never talked about her, and they were kind enough not to mention her name to me."

"What was her name?" Ava asked.

"Gui-San — Lin Gui-San," he said.

"You don't have to tell me anything about her that makes you uncomfortable."

"She was very beautiful and brave...like you," he said. "I'll never forgive myself for what happened to her."

"You don't have to go on," Ava said.

Uncle shook his head. "About halfway across the bay, we realized we had lost one of our people. But it was too late to turn back, so we kept swimming. Gui-San asked me to stay close to her, and I tried. Then I was hit by a wave and swallowed a mouthful of that foul water. Minutes later I was so ill that I had to be taken out of the water and put on the raft. I stayed there until we reached Yuen Long. When we were safely on land, I started to regain my senses and asked to see Gui-San," Uncle said, closing his eyes. "She wasn't there. We had lost her and one other during the last part of the swim. It would never have happened if I had stayed close to her. She died because I failed her."

Uncle heard Ava begin to sob. He opened his eyes and saw tears trickling down her cheeks.

"Now you know my secret, Ava, and there's no need ever to talk about it again," he whispered.

"It wasn't your fault," she said, ignoring his request. "That could have happened to anyone."

"Except it happened to me, and it cost Gui-San her life," he said, and paused. "But my good memories of her are still vivid, and during times of crisis in my life those thoughts have sustained me. I believe that she is waiting for me on the other side and that I'll see her again."

"I will pray that you do."

"Well, maybe between your prayers and my prayers we can make it happen," he said. "Now, I want to discuss funeral arrangements with you."

"I don't want to go over them again," Ava said, gathering herself. "I know you want to keep things simple, Uncle. No public announcement. No elaborate ceremonies. Just a short viewing at the funeral home."

"There is something else."

"What is it?"

"I want you to arrange for some monks to be at the gravesite in Fanling. They do not have to be at the funeral home, but I want them at the grave. There should be five of them. Uncle Fong can help you contact the right person."

A look of surprise crossed Ava's face.

"I want Taoist monks because that was my parents' way, and I feel a need to honour them and their traditions. It may also bring me closer to my ancestors."

"I'll speak to Uncle Fong. We'll look after it," she said.

"One more thing about Fong. He still knows a lot of the old contacts, and I told him that if you ever need help that he is to act as if he were me, and to invoke my name if it comes to that."

"Uncle, I'm not going back into the old business. I won't need those types of contacts anymore."

He stared at her. "I know your new business is different and that May Ling has *guanxi*, but there may still be times when you need other kinds of help. I want to make sure it will always be available to you."

"Yes, Uncle," she said.

"Good. I do not want to have to worry about you."

"You don't need to worry."

"Thank you, my beautiful girl. Now, where is Sonny? I need to speak to him."

"He's outside. I'll get him. They only allow one visitor at a time in the room, so I'll wait outside until you're finished with him."

"I only need him for a minute."

Uncle watched Ava leave and felt a sense of relief. He had been worried about how she would react when he told her about Gui-San. Given how close they were, and despite how much they respected each other's privacy, it was an awfully big secret to have kept from her. But it had gone well, he thought, and now she was there to help Fong if he had any problems with the Ancestor Worship Hall in Yuen Long.

Sonny entered the room with an odd expression on his face.

"Don't look so glum. I'm not dead yet, and Parker thinks I'll have more time if I take better care of myself," Uncle said.

"We all want you to do that," said Sonny.

"You may have to help me more than usual over the next few days. I've decided to go to Shanghai to see Xu. I want you to come with me."

"Whatever you want, boss."

"I'll tell Ava I'm going, but I'm not ready to tell her about Xu, so keep that quiet," Uncle said. "I need to clarify things with him before I introduce them to each other. So until I tell you otherwise, not one word."

"Not one word," Sonny repeated.

"Good. Now ask Ava to come back."

When she returned, Uncle smiled at her. "I just promised Sonny that I would go back on my congee diet."

"That will make everyone happy."

"I have a reason, though, that goes beyond my immediate health."

"Do I want to hear what it is?" she asked.

"I have to go to Shanghai."

"Shanghai?"

"Do not look so alarmed. It is only a two-hour flight."

"But Shanghai?"

"I have some business there to attend to. Sonny will travel with me."

"Business?" Ava asked, sounding surprised.

"It is something I can't discuss with you just now. I gave my word to the other party that no one else would be involved."

"You're taking Sonny."

"To carry and drive, nothing more."

"Uncle, this is so strange. Is it some piece of unfinished triad business?"

"I can't discuss it," he said, reaching for her hand. "All I can tell you is that when I received the invitation to go it made me very happy. In fact, it made me rather excited, which was one reason I ate and drank like a fool last night. Ava, this does not concern any business we have ever done or people you have ever met. If it did, I would take you with me. Besides, it will give you a break. With the wedding over and me away for a few days, you can have some time to yourself."

"How long will you be gone?"

"Two or three days, no more."

"Uncle —"

"Please do not argue with me about this."

"If there's any problem?"

"Someone will call you, I promise."

3

UNCLE FELT MUCH BETTER THE NEXT MORNING AND hoped to be released from the hospital. But Parker had other ideas.

"If you insist on travelling to Shanghai, I want to make sure you're strong enough before you leave here," he said. "I want you to stay for another day."

Uncle saw no benefit in arguing. He knew Sonny would be waiting to hear when he could come get him, so that was the first phone call he made.

"I'll be here for another day. It is a precaution, nothing more. But I want you to do something for me," Uncle said to Sonny. "The form for today's races at Sha Tin is at the apartment. Could you get it for me? I'll place my bets by phone."

"Sure, boss."

Uncle was preparing to call Ava next when his phone rang. He saw a familiar Chinese area code, but an unfamiliar number. "*Wei*," he answered.

"Uncle, this is Wong Changxing," May Ling's husband said.

Uncle and Changxing had known each other for many years, but rarely exchanged phone calls. Uncle immediately wondered what had prompted this one. "How are you, Changxing? Ava told me that you were coming to Hong Kong with May Ling for Amanda Yee's wedding. Are you in town?"

"I am, and I had to call when I heard from May Ling that you had an unfortunate medical issue last night. From the sound of your voice, I trust everything is okay now?"

"It seems to be."

"That's great to hear. We can't afford to lose a man like you."

"We are all going to go someday, Changxing. It doesn't matter how much money or power you have, you can't beat time," said Uncle.

"But you can always buy a little more, and I hope you have."

Uncle sighed. He didn't know why Changxing had called him, but he was sure it wasn't to exchange platitudes. "Thank you for calling and for your kindness. Enjoy the rest of your stay in Hong Kong," he said.

Changxing hesitated and then said, "Just one minute. There is something else I wanted to discuss with you."

"I am listening."

"Well, I'm wondering if Ava has discussed the business problem that she and May have encountered in Borneo."

"No, she hasn't. I'm not aware of any problem, and I also don't know anything about their business in Borneo or elsewhere."

"I wish she had. It has May on edge, so I suspect a lot of money is involved," Changxing said. "I would like to help, but she won't discuss it with me. Perhaps if you asked Ava about it, she'd be more open?"

"To what end? It seems to me that the women are quite intent on creating their own business. Ava certainly doesn't need my input, and May might not want or need yours. Perhaps the best thing to do is to let them get on with things."

"And lose millions?"

"It is their money to lose."

Changxing went quiet.

"And my understanding is that May is still working in your businesses. You might not be getting her total attention, but she hasn't abandoned you."

"That's true, but I don't like the idea of her being distracted."

"My advice is not to interfere with what they're trying to do. Whether you are right or wrong, no one will thank you for it," Uncle said pointedly. "If I were you, I would tell May that you support her whatever she chooses to do, and that you are there for her if she needs you."

"All I want to know is the nature and size of the problem they have. That is hardly interference."

"Then you'll have to get that information from May because I won't ask Ava, and even if she decides to volunteer the information, I'm not going to pass it to you or anyone else."

Changxing sighed in frustration. Uncle knew he was a man accustomed to getting his way and braced himself for an outburst. But to his surprise, the so-called Emperor of Hubei simply said, "I won't get it from May. She is too proud and stubborn."

"I don't know what else to tell you," said Uncle.

"There is nothing to say. I guess there are some things I'm going to have to accept," Changxing said. "Anyway, thanks for listening and for the advice, Uncle. Stay well."

Uncle put down the phone and leaned back on his pillow. He thought about Changxing and felt some sympathy. After all those years of May Ling being devoted to him and their businesses, he was obviously struggling with the fact that she wanted to make changes that did not include him. Uncle also felt a touch of guilt for having urged Ava to join forces with May, although he was sure that his encouragement hadn't been the reason she eventually did. As he contemplated the complexities involved in dealing with strong, independent women, his eyes began to close.

He wasn't aware he'd fallen asleep until he heard his name. Uncle opened his eyes to see Sonny talking to a nurse in the doorway to his room. "What's going on?" he asked.

"Your friend is trying to visit outside of regular hours. I was told it was allowed last night, but those were exceptional circumstances. That isn't the case now, and I've just told your friend he has to come back later."

"Do what the nurse tells you," Uncle said to Sonny.

"But I have your racing form," he said.

"I will take it and give it to him," the nurse said to Sonny.

"Off you go. I'll see you later," Uncle said. "But call Fong for me, will you, and tell him I'll be phoning my bets into Dong's. I'm not sure how much I have in my account there, so ask Fong to keep it topped at fifty thousand."

"Okay," Sonny said, then turned and left.

"Here you are," the nurse said, handing Uncle the racing form.

He sat up, drank from a glass of water, and opened it. He wasn't sure how his concentration would be, but as he reviewed the work he'd done on previous days, he had no trouble following it. He was on the fifth race when his phone rang. He thought briefly about not answering until he saw Ava's name.

"How are you feeling?" she asked.

"Much better, but Parker will not let me out of here until tomorrow."

"Thank God someone is being sensible."

"I know better than to argue with him."

"Do you want me to drop by?" she asked.

"No, there is no need today. I'll be focused on the races at Sha Tin. I'll rent a television for the day."

"What would you do without horse racing?"

"I hope I never have to find out," he laughed.

"You do sound better, but I was thinking about you wanting to go to Shanghai. Are you sure you're strong enough?"

"Parker is keeping me here for an extra day so he can make sure I am."

"When will you leave?" Ava asked.

"Tomorrow night, or maybe the next morning."

"In that case," Ava said slowly, "if you aren't going to be in Hong Kong, then I may take a trip as well."

"That sounds like an excellent idea," he said. "But tell me, would it have anything to do with the problem you have in Borneo?"

"I beg your pardon," Ava said, her surprise audible.

Uncle hesitated and wondered if he had spoken out of turn. *What the hell*, he thought, and asked, "Have you spoken to May Ling since the wedding?"

"She's sitting right in front of me. Why do you ask?"

"Changxing."

"What about him?"

"He called me a few hours ago to see how I was doing.

But what he really wanted was to ask if you had discussed some business problem with me that he thought you and May were having in Borneo."

"Why would he do that?" she asked.

Uncle could hear annoyance in her voice, but knew it wasn't directed at him. "I don't know."

"Well, it's true, there is a problem, but it has nothing to do with him."

"Or me, and I made that clear," Uncle said. "But he did infer a lot of money might be involved, and that you and May might be exposed."

"It does involve a lot of money, and there is substantial risk."

"Can you sort things out?"

"Maybe. May and Amanda are getting ready to leave for Borneo, but part of our problem is in the Netherlands, and I should go there. Now that I know your plans, I will try to leave for Amsterdam tonight if I can get a flight."

"Ava, you do not have to tell me, but how much money do you stand to lose personally?"

"The business could lose between twenty and thirty million U.S. dollars," she said without hesitation.

"No wonder Changxing was so eager for details."

"We have the money."

"Still."

"Uncle, I'm fine."

"That may be true, but it doesn't stop me worrying about you and your future," he said. "Look, when you get back from Amsterdam, I want you to meet with my lawyer, Peter Hutchinson. I know I have gone over the basics of my will with you, but I would like Peter to lay out all the details.

There are a few provisions that I have not described. You need to be aware of them, and Hutchinson will be only too pleased to answer any questions you have about anything in my will."

"Okay," Ava said with a hint of reluctance. "But I have to settle this business in Borneo first. I'll meet with him as soon as that's done and I'm back in Hong Kong."

"Thank you, Ava."

"Uncle, I have to go now. May and I have to get organized before we leave," she said. "I will be available to you any time, night or day, so if there's a change in your plans or if there are any problems, I want you to let me know right away. You are my number one priority."

Uncle felt tears well in his eyes as he put down the phone. Was there a luckier man in Hong Kong?

4

PARKER CAME TO SEE HIM THE NEXT MORNING AT eleven.

"How did you sleep?" the doctor asked.

"Very well."

"I saw that you ate breakfast this morning. Was there any unpleasant reaction?"

"None, I feel fine."

"And now, the most important question of all," Parker said. "How did you do with the races at Sha Tin yesterday?"

Uncle grimaced. "I had the worst day I've had in years. I didn't win a single race, and the harder I tried to recoup, the worse my luck seemed to get."

"Well, I can't make up for that, but I can give you some good news: you're free to go home if you still want to go."

"You know I do, and you also know I intend to go to Shanghai as soon as possible."

"I'm not crazy about that idea, but I won't stand in your way as long as you promise to practise moderation in all things."

"You have my word, doctor."

"Then I'll tell the nurses you're free to go."

Uncle phoned Sonny as soon as Parker left the room. "Come and get me," he said.

His next call was to Shanghai. Xu's housekeeper answered the phone, and although she was younger than Uncle, he referred to her as everyone else did. "Auntie Grace, it is Uncle. I'd like to speak to Xu if he's available."

"For you he is always available. Wait just a minute," she said.

"Uncle, how are you?" Xu asked less than a minute later.

"I'm ready to travel. I'm thinking I'll come to Shanghai either tonight or tomorrow. What works best for you?"

"I have a meeting tonight that I shouldn't cancel, so tomorrow is best."

"Then tomorrow it is."

"Call me with your flight details. My day is relatively open so I should be able to meet you at the airport," Xu said. "I will book a suite for you at the Peninsula. Will Sonny be with you?"

"Yes."

"I'll get him a room as well."

"That's perfect. See you tomorrow," said Uncle.

He thought about calling his travel agent, but suddenly felt weary. He lay back on the bed to wait for Sonny. He decided he would also take it easy when he got back to the apartment. His trips to Shanghai were usually busy with meetings and visits to Xu's various businesses. He was intimately familiar with everything Xu had done, was doing, and planned to do. His advice wasn't always taken, but it was never dismissed out of hand.

How many more trips will there be to Shanghai? He had

asked that question many times over the past several weeks, and wishful thinking aside, the answer was that this was probably going to be the last. Xu knew that Uncle hadn't been feeling terrific, but not that he was seriously ill. That would have to be made clear. Once it was, Uncle would speak to Xu about Ava, and if that went well — and he saw no reason it wouldn't — he would talk to her about Xu when he got back to Hong Kong.

"Hey, boss," Sonny said from the doorway.

"How did you get here so soon?" Uncle asked.

"No faster than normal."

Uncle blinked, then realized he had been daydreaming. "Of course not. Let's get me out of here."

Fifteen minutes later Uncle sat in the back seat of the Mercedes for the short trip to his apartment.

"We are going to Shanghai tomorrow. I'll book the one o'clock flight. You can pick me up around ten," Uncle said as Sonny eased the car into traffic.

"How long will we be there?"

"Two days, maybe three. It will depend on what Xu has planned, and I have some things I need to discuss with him."

"Have you told Ava you're going?"

"Yes, and as it turns out, she won't be in Hong Kong for the next few days anyway. She and May have a business problem that needs to be addressed. Ava is planning to go to Amsterdam, and may even have left last night."

"It sounds funny to hear you speak about Ava and May as partners," said Sonny.

"Does it bother you?"

"To be honest, it kind of scares me," Sonny said, glancing in the rear-view mirror at Uncle. "We've always been a great team."

"Are you afraid that when I'm gone Ava will move on?"

"She'll have May Ling and Amanda Yee."

"Has Ava discussed her plans with you?" Uncle asked.

"No."

"I'm surprised, because she talked to me," he said. "She made it clear that she wants you to work for her."

"She's going to move to Hong Kong?"

"No, but she expects to spend time here. When she is in town, she'll want you to do for her what you have been doing for me," said Uncle, and then saw a look of confusion cross Sonny's face. "And when she's not here, she told me that she would like you to drive for her father, and her half-brother Michael. She would also like you to keep a protective eye on them and Amanda Yee. She doesn't want a repeat of what happened in Macau."

"She hasn't mentioned a word of this to me," Sonny said, sounding not quite convinced.

"I am sure she's just been waiting for the right moment. Maybe she thought talking about it too soon would be bad luck where I'm concerned," Uncle said. "I'll tell her we had this conversation and that she should talk to you directly."

"It is good to know she has plans for me, but there's no need for her to tell me about them just yet," said Sonny. "You are going to be around for a long time."

Uncle started to reply and then caught himself. With or without him, the world would keep moving. The best he could do was to leave a legacy, and what greater legacy could there be than the bridges he had built between the people who were most important in his life.

5

THE CATHAY PACIFIC FLIGHT LANDED IN SHANGHAI THE next day on schedule, and when Uncle and Sonny walked through the arrivals door at Hongqiao International Airport, he saw Xu waiting for them. There was a large crowd, but Xu was easy to identify in a black suit and a white shirt with a silk black tie. He had started wearing those clothes after becoming Mountain Master. Uncle hadn't known how to react. In one way it was a compliment, but in another he was afraid Xu would be mocked for copying the way Uncle dressed. He needn't have worried. Xu had such an air of sophistication and purpose about him that it defied anything but respect in return.

"Uncle, so good to see you. It has been too long," Xu said, stepping forward with his hand extended.

Uncle held it for longer than any handshake demanded. He looked up at his protégé and smiled. Xu was close to six foot, lean, and like his father had a thick head of hair that he wore slicked back. He had inherited his looks, however, from his mother. Whereas Xu the elder's face had been almost round, with a pug nose and a small chin, the younger Xu's was more sharply defined, with a thin nose, a square jaw, and sharp cheekbones. It would have been a harsh face, if not for his large eyes that were generally soft and welcoming but could turn ice-cold if the situation demanded it.

"Good to see you too," Uncle said, and then nodded at the man who stood next to Xu. He was a few inches taller than Sonny and as thick across the chest. His name was Suen, Xu's Red Pole — the man who ran the gang's troops on the ground.

"You're looking well," Xu said.

"Looks can be deceiving," said Uncle.

Xu shook his head. "Don't alarm me. I can't afford to lose you."

"I didn't mean anything by it," Uncle said, noticing that Sonny was avoiding looking at them. "What is our itinerary?"

"I'll tell you about it when we get to the car," said Xu.

The four men made their way through the throng in the arrivals hall. Suen and Sonny walked side by side in front, forming a moving wall. The car was on the sixth level of a parking garage, and Uncle was grateful there was an elevator. As much as he thought he had been conserving his energy all day, he suspected it wouldn't take much to tire him.

Xu's car was a black Mercedes-Benz S-Class and was typically driven by a forty-niner, but there was no sign of a driver. Suen opened the back doors for Uncle and Xu, opened the trunk for Sonny to stow the bags, then climbed into the driver's seat with Sonny sitting next to him.

Uncle knew it was only a twenty-kilometre drive from the airport to the Peninsula Hotel, which was located on the world-famous Bund, but he also knew Shanghai traffic was unpredictable. Their ride could take anywhere from fifteen minutes to more than an hour.

"I wanted you to come to the house for dinner tonight, but Yan — the Mountain Master from Wuxi — has been pushing for a meeting. I've been putting him off," Xu said as they left the garage. "I wasn't sure how long you planned to stay, and since tomorrow night I have a long-standing commitment with Fu from Suzhou, I thought I'd try to fit in Yan tonight. Are you okay with that?"

"What does Yan want?"

"Marketing and distribution support," said Xu. "He's making knock-off handbags and shoes, but there's stiff competition from the other gangs, and he's hoping to tap into our network."

Uncle nodded. "Fine, we'll meet."

"I thought, since you are at the Peninsula, we could eat at Yi Long Court. I had dinner there last month and it was terrific."

"In terms of food, it makes no difference to me where we eat, but I do like the idea of being at the hotel."

"Good, and then tomorrow we'll go to Nantong. I want you to see the new phone factory, and meet some of the technical people we hired away from Apple. They are telling me that we should be getting into laptop computers, but I'm a bit concerned that it may raise our profile too much. The last thing we need is to attract unnecessary government attention."

"As I remember it, you have partners from government in that factory."

"We do, but they are very nervous these days."

"Why?"

"The Premier has launched another anti-corruption campaign, and he has turned the Central Commission for

Discipline Inspection loose again. They are targeting his political rivals but they tend to cast their net quite wide. No one knows who could get caught up in it. And once you're caught, there is no way to extract yourself. Even if you have done nothing, they'll find something for you to confess to."

"Then why consider laptops?"

"The profit margins are twice those of phones."

They were nearing the Huangpu River and traffic became stop-and-go. "I think I'd like to rest when we get to the hotel," Uncle said.

"Of course, we'll see you checked in and I'll come back later. Our dinner reservation is at seven, so I'll be at the hotel by quarter to the hour."

It was almost five by the time Uncle reached his suite. He unpacked the small bag he'd brought and thought briefly about napping before deciding he wasn't really that tired. He opened a bottle of water and was about to turn on the television when there was a knock at the door. He looked through the eyehole and saw Sonny.

"Is there a problem?" he asked, opening the door.

"I tried to call your cell, but it isn't on," Sonny said. "I just opened mine and it has a message from Ava. She says she has been trying to reach you. She sounds worried."

"I haven't had my phone on since I left the apartment," Uncle said, immediately angry at himself. "Did she say why she was calling?"

"No, only that she was trying to reach you and couldn't. She told me to tell you to call her as soon as possible. I'm sure there's a message on your phone as well. Maybe it has more detail."

"I'll check," Uncle said. "If I need you, I'll let you know."

Uncle went immediately to his jacket and found his phone in a pocket. There was only one message. It had been left at two, when Uncle was in the air, which made him feel slightly less irresponsible. He sat on a couch to listen to it.

"Uncle, this is Ava. I'm at the airport in Amsterdam. I need to speak to you. I'd love to hear from you in the next half hour or so, but if that's not possible, please keep your phone on," she said.

She sounded distressed. Surely not being able to contact him couldn't be the cause of it. Had something gone wrong on her trip? Had May run into further problems in Borneo? He thought of these scenarios in quick succession as he called her number — only to be immediately put through to her voicemail. She's in mid-air, he thought, as he said, "I got your message. My phone has been off most of the day. I'm sorry about that. Call me when you can. I'll make sure I'm available. And by the way, I'm feeling fine, if that's one of your concerns."

I shouldn't have made that last comment, he thought as he put down the phone. It made him appear self-absorbed when whatever was causing her distress probably had nothing to do with him. He finished drinking the water and walked to the window that overlooked the Huangpu River. The Peninsula was one of fifty-two buildings that comprised the Bund. They were an eclectic mix that included colonial architecture as well as a large number of buildings — like the Peninsula — designed in the art deco style. They were part of old Shanghai, and one of the few areas to survive the determination of successive city governments to tear down everything that had existed pre-Mao and replace them with something newer, shinier, and larger.

Uncle had seen massive changes in China during his lifetime. He had witnessed first-hand the rapid growth of the Shenzhen Special Economic Zone from a sleepy market town with a population of thirty-five thousand to a world-class economic powerhouse with over ten million residents. But even that didn't compare to what had gone on in Shanghai. When Xu the elder had first resettled there, Pudong — the side of the Huangpu River across from the Bund — was mainly farmland. Now Pudong's Lujiazui district was home to thirty skyscrapers and towers that took turns being China's tallest building. The most recent addition was the Shanghai Tower, which — at 632 metres and with 128 storeys — was now the second tallest in the world. As astounding to Uncle was the city's population explosion. In 1990 it was about nine million, and now it was twenty-four million, and it was predicted to soar past thirty million in a few years. If nothing else, that size provided Xu with endless opportunities to make money, and to stay under the radar while he did.

Uncle remained at the window for several minutes, staring at the Huangpu and its surroundings, before moving back into the living room. He turned on the television and went back and forth between news programs and a variety show. Nothing really held his attention as his mind wandered between Ava and the conversation he needed to have with Xu.

At six-forty, he left the room and took the elevator to the lobby. When he emerged, he saw Xu talking to a short, stout man wearing a grey suit, a white shirt, and a blue Gucci tie. Uncle guessed he was Yan, and couldn't help but wonder if the tie was a knock-off. Off to one side, Suen stood with a man Uncle recognized as one of Xu's forty-niners, and two other men he assumed were with Yan. The contrast between Xu's and Yan's men was striking. Xu did not like his men to be visibly tattooed, have outlandish hairstyles, or dress in a manner that drew attention to themselves. Dressed in slacks and polo shirts and with their hair cropped short, Suen and the Shanghai forty-niner typified the look Xu wanted. Yan's men, on the other hand, wore jeans and T-shirts, and both were heavily tattooed.

"Uncle, right on time as usual," Xu said when he saw him. "Let me introduce you to Yan, the Mountain Master of Wuxi."

Yan stepped forward and lowered his head. "What a privilege it is to meet you. I could scarcely believe my good luck when Xu told me you would be dining with us tonight."

"You are very kind," Uncle said.

"And you are a legend."

Uncle shook his head. "I'm a brother like you who happened to be in the right place at the right time on a few occasions during my career."

"That's only a small part of the truth. But let's not embarrass Uncle anymore," Xu said, glancing at his watch. "We are a little early for dinner, but I think they'll seat us."

Suen left the men he was with and approached Xu. "We'll be having dinner at the Compass Bar on the ground floor, so we're close if you need us," he said, and turned to Uncle. "We've asked Sonny to join us."

"Thank you."

"Then let's go upstairs," Xu said.

Yi Long Court was on the second floor of the hotel. It had a traditional, classic design with a dark wooden floor, tables covered in white linen, and carved wooden chairs padded with red leather. They were led to a table that afforded some privacy, near the back of the restaurant.

"I'm going to start with Scotch," Xu said as they sat. "What will you have?"

"A Tsingtao," said Yan.

"Water," said Uncle.

"That's unusual," said Xu.

"I've been having some stomach issues. I'll explain later," Uncle said.

"Will it affect what you can eat?"

"I can't have anything too spicy, but otherwise I should be okay."

After the server left with their drink orders, Xu turned to Yan. "I asked Uncle to join us tonight because he has been advising me on business issues for some years now. It isn't something that's commonly known, but it isn't a secret either."

"You are fortunate to have such a sage advisor. I know he was the one who opened the door for the society to return to China, and I know he taught many Mountain Masters — including my predecessor — how to coexist with the Communists."

"Xu has explained to me that you want to use his marketing and distribution networks for your goods," Uncle said, ignoring the compliment. "Could you go into more detail? For example, I'd like to know exactly what you are manufacturing, and why you are having problems taking your goods to market yourself."

For the next hour and a half, in between enjoying small portions of double boiled bamboo fungus in a matsutake clear broth and poached marble grade beef, Uncle listened to Yan explain why and how he had gotten into the knock-off luxury leather goods business, and the details of the challenges he faced. Yan finished just as the dessert of sweetened almond cream with egg whites was served.

Uncle had eaten carefully — acutely sensitive to any change in his body. At all times, he was prepared to stop eating and leave the table if he felt the slightest discomfort. But he made it to the almond cream without a disruption, and it went down beautifully.

Yan had done more talking than eating, and also more drinking. He finished three Tsingtao beers by the time dessert was served, and both he and Xu ordered cognac to finish their meal. Uncle had asked a few questions during Yan's exposition but had mainly stayed quiet, listening. When the table was cleared of everything but Uncle's glass of water and the two cognacs, Uncle said to Yan, "I apologize if you think this is rude, but it seems to me that you have gone about things in reverse order."

"How so?" Yan asked, in a curious rather than offended manner.

"Well, you put millions of dollars into constructing a first-class factory; you hired the best artisans you could find; and you took the time to create a reliable supply line for your raw materials. What you should have done first was figure out what the market wanted and where you could fit into it."

"The market wants Fendi, Gucci, Hermès, Louis Vuitton, and Prada. We make them all."

"And the problem with that is I know of at least three other factories owned by rival gangs making those exact products, and they are already in place and dominating the markets you want to enter," Xu said. "To break in you'll have to take them on, which could lead to price wars ... or worse."

"I'm aware," Yan said. "A container of bags we shipped to Guangzhou last month was hijacked and the contents destroyed."

Uncle leaned towards Yan. "My dear friend, even if Xu gives you access to his distribution network, the result might not be any different."

"And by taking your goods on, I would risk angering some very good customers," said Xu.

"So what am I supposed to do? The two of you make it sound like I'm in a hopeless situation."

"I don't believe you are," said Uncle. "I have a suggestion if you care to hear it."

"You have my full attention."

"From what you've told me, your factory is capable of copying any leather manufacturer in the world. Is that true?"

"Given enough time and the right materials, my people can come close."

"Then avoid the low-hanging fruit. Don't make Prada or Hermès or Louis Vuitton. There have to be other brands that your competitors aren't making. Find some that may not have wide customer recognition but fill a niche, and perhaps have the potential to grow. Offhand, can you think of any?"

Yan looked thoughtful, then said, "There are some."

"If that's the case, then you have the opportunity to create new product lines that won't be in direct competition with the other factories."

"I'm still left with the problem of marketing and distribution."

"Go to your competitors, and either sell directly to them

or work out a deal that lets you use their distribution systems," said Uncle, smiling. "All of a sudden you wouldn't be a threat to them; your new product lines would be an asset they can add to their own business."

"I have done deals like that with my phones," Xu said to Yan. "Whenever a genuine competitor appears on the horizon, I meet with them and make it clear that they have a choice — they can try to compete with me, or join forces. If they want to compete, I tell them that if I have to, I'll give my phones away to maintain my market position. But if they sell me their product, their phones will always have a home, and their profit margins will be secure. Thus far, no one has chosen the first option, and I have been able to increase my volume without having to invest a single dollar."

"It does make sense," Yan said, shaking his head. "I'm kicking myself for not thinking of it myself. It would have saved me months of worry and a lot of money."

"You would have got there eventually," Xu said.

"I can't thank you both enough for this," Yan said, looking at his watch. "But I have already taken up enough of your time. Let me pay for dinner and I'll head home to Wuxi."

"Keep us posted on how you're doing, and don't hesitate to call me if you want to talk," Xu said.

Five minutes later the three men left Yi Long Court and descended the staircase to the lobby. Suen, Sonny, and the others were already there. Goodbyes were said, and Xu and Uncle lingered as Yan left the hotel.

"It's been a long day for you," Xu said. "I should let you go to your suite now."

"I will go to the suite, but I would like it if you came with me," Uncle said. "There are some matters we need to discuss."

"HELP YOURSELF TO THE MINIBAR," UNCLE SAID AS THEY entered the suite. "There's some good Scotch in there."

"Will you be sticking to water?"

"No, since it is just the two of us, I think I'll try a beer."

"Uncle, I have to say that you're alarming me with all this talk about your health."

"It is a subject that can't be avoided," Uncle said, opening a bottle of Tsingtao. "Let's sit at the table."

A look of confusion crossed Xu's face, and Uncle realized this was not going to be easy.

Xu carried a small bottle of Johnnie Walker Black Label to the table and poured it into a glass. "What kind of health problem are you having?" he asked.

"To put it bluntly, I'm dying," Uncle said forcefully.

"What!"

"I have stomach cancer that has spread to some vital organs and is inoperable," Uncle said. "When it was discovered last fall, my doctor recommended chemotherapy to buy me a little more time. I tried it, but the treatment was worse than the disease, so I stopped."

"How long have you known?"

"A few months. It wasn't something I could tell you over the phone. I wanted to do it like this, face to face," said Uncle, taking several sips of beer. "Now, I know you are upset, but I'm an old man who has lived a good life. And I'm fortunate now to leave it with things in order."

Xu emptied his glass of Scotch in two large gulps. "Upset is an understatement. This is devastating," he said, slowly shaking his head. "I know you are at an age, Uncle, but I've never thought of you as being old. I've always thought you — like Auntie Grace — were a permanent part of my life."

"I wish that was the case, but it isn't, and so we have to deal with it."

Xu went to the minibar to get another drink. "And there is absolutely nothing that can be done about this? There isn't a clinic somewhere else that can help?"

"No, there isn't. I've been fortunate to have a doctor in Hong Kong who is honest with me. He made my situation quite clear," said Uncle.

Xu lowered his eyes, and Uncle thought he saw tears in them.

"I've had time to put things in order in Hong Kong," he continued. "Funeral and burial arrangements are set. My will has been finalized. And everyone there who I felt needed to know has been told."

"How many people is that?"

"Only a handful — Fong, Sonny, my housekeeper, my partner Ava, and I believe she told her partners. I trust them all to keep my secret, and I trust you to do the same. I do not want anyone else to know."

"Uncle, I would never go against your wishes, but shouldn't

the society be given the opportunity to honour you?"

"They can honour me when I'm dead."

"And they will," Xu said, his voice breaking slightly.

"That doesn't matter. My immediate concern is putting things in order. Hong Kong is done, and that leaves Shanghai," he said, pausing to sip again. "I have a favour to ask of you, Xu. Two favours, in fact."

"Anything."

"Don't say that so quickly."

"Just tell me what you need from me."

Uncle paused again as he gathered his thoughts. "First, I want you to run for the chairmanship of the Heaven and Earth Society," he said slowly. "We've discussed it before, and you know how strongly I believe the society needs your leadership. While you've never said no to my request, I can't help thinking you are simply humouring me."

"I would never do that. I haven't said yes because it isn't an easy decision to make."

"I know, but most things that are worthwhile do not come easily," said Uncle. "I remember when your father made the decision to move back to Shanghai. He was torn between returning to his home, and enduring all the risks and hardships that entailed, or staying in Fanling in relative comfort and security. His choice opened the door for the society to return to China after years of banishment. He put the brotherhood ahead of his self-interest. I'm asking you to do the same."

"I have so much at stake here, so many people depending on me."

"You don't have to abandon them. Ideally, the chairmanship shouldn't demand your full attention. It was primarily established to resolve disputes among gangs over territory and businesses, so if there are no disputes the demands are minimal."

"But right now, many gangs are at each other's throats."

"That's why we need you. The current chairman does nothing. He has forgotten the chairman's role. We have warring gangs, which draws unwanted attention from the police and military, hurts our businesses, and ultimately hurts the brethren. We need to re-establish peace in the brotherhood. You have the respect to make that happen."

"I'll be opposed. There are Mountain Masters who don't like interference of any kind; there are Mountain Masters — like the current chairman — who prefer chaos."

"It was the same when I was chairman, but I was able to make it work. Always remember, there is no substitute for having more firepower. The road to peace comes easiest when your enemies understand your strength and believe you'll use it if you have to."

"People doing the right thing for the wrong reason," Xu said with a smile. "That is the lesson my father drummed into me."

"Yes, and you can rarely go wrong behaving accordingly." Uncle took another sip of beer. "Coming back to your responsibilities in Shanghai," he said. "I remained Mountain Master in Fanling when I became chairman. I delegated some of my jobs to my executive team, which worked out well. Do you trust your people?"

"Of course, they're all capable and loyal to me and the gang."

"Then there is no reason for you not to say yes."

"Apparently not."

"Then you will run?"

Xu paused and then said, "Yes, Uncle, assuming nothing happens in Shanghai that would force me to change my mind, I will run."

"Thank you, Xu."

"But I have to say, without you as my advisor, I will feel lost. There is no one else I trust so completely."

Uncle felt a weight leave his chest. Was this fate intervening to make his next request easier? "Actually, there is someone. You just haven't met her yet," he said.

"*Her*?"

"My partner, Ava Lee."

7

XU'S LIPS PRESSED TOGETHER AND HIS BROW FURROWED slightly. It was his way of expressing doubt — a signal that he needed to be convinced. Uncle decided to take a different approach.

"I have mentioned Ava to you several times over the years, but I have never spoken about the kind of person she is and the relationship we have," he said. "Do you care to listen?"

"Of course."

"Do you want to get another Scotch before I begin?"

"Sure."

"Good, then you can bring me another beer. All this talking is thirsty work."

"Are you sure you can handle it?"

"I'll drink it slowly."

When Xu returned, Uncle emptied his first beer and thanked him for the second. Xu put a small bottle each of Scotch and cognac on the table.

"Let me start with the facts," Uncle began. "Ava is a forensic accountant. She was born in Hong Kong, the second daughter of a second wife who was sent to Canada with her children when she became troublesome. So Ava was raised in Canada, but speaks fluent Cantonese and Mandarin, as well as English. She is in her mid-thirties —"

"I didn't know she was so young," Xu interrupted. "How old was she when you became partners?"

"She was in her mid-twenties. That astounded many of my friends in Hong Kong, including Fong, but they quickly realized she is capable beyond her years," said Uncle. "Of course, there were rumours at the beginning, gossip about an old man and a beautiful young woman. But there was nothing to them. Ava isn't interested in men."

"She told you this?"

"Not directly, but we've worked together closely for the last decade —"

"And you are alert to what's going on around you," Xu said.

"A trait that both you and Ava share."

"Let's not talk about me. I'd like to hear more about her."

"Yes," Uncle said, pleased with the request. "Well, she is very intelligent, and not just with numbers. She reads people as well as anyone I've ever known. Over the years, I have learned to trust her judgement completely in that regard. She is loyal to her friends, determined to finish whatever she starts, and fearless — though she recognizes danger when she sees it."

"I don't normally equate accountancy with danger," Xu said.

"The debt collection business is not for the faint of heart. Ava is an expert at locating stolen money. But once she's found it, it's rare that someone returns it voluntarily. They have to be persuaded, and Ava has become adept at pushing the right buttons. Sometimes they respond with violence. Ava's been punched, shot at, threatened with knives, and faced other threats she hasn't discussed with me."

"And she can handle that?"

"More than handle, she is a martial arts expert. I've seen her take down men twice her size."

"She sounds like an impressive woman," Xu said.

"She is . . . and I love her. I'd lay down my life for her, and she'd do the same for me," Uncle said, his voice rising as his emotions took over. "She is the granddaughter I never had."

Uncle saw Xu's surprise at his candour. "I'm telling you this for two reasons," Uncle continued before Xu could speak. "The first, as I suggested, is that I believe Ava would be a terrific confidante and advisor for you. You could tell her anything and know that it would be kept private. In return, she would give you her honest and thoughtful opinion. The second reason is that, when I'm gone, I want her to have someone she can call on for help and advice if she needs it. I know that she's getting out of the debt collection business, but she will still be doing business in Asia, and you know how difficult that can be. She is partnering with May Ling Wong —"

"The May Ling Wong from Wuhan, the wife of Wong Changxing?"

"Yes, they've formed a company with Ava's sister-in-law, Amanda Yee, called the Three Sisters, which they've capitalized with two hundred million U.S."

"Is May Ling cutting ties with Changxing?"

"No, she'll retain her interest in their businesses, but she and Ava have decided to build their own empire."

"That is very interesting," Xu said.

Uncle sensed an opening to discuss the possibility of the Shanghai gang putting money into the Three Sisters, but decided it should be a separate conversation.

"But even with May's involvement, there will be times when Ava will need the type of assistance that only my triad links could provide. You are the person I would like her to call on when I am gone," said Uncle. "In my mind, and as strange as it might sound, I have thought of you almost as brother and sister. I know it is late to bring you together, but the timing never seemed right until now."

Xu held his glass between his palms and stared at Uncle. "This has been a conversation filled with surprises," he said finally.

"I know, and I apologize for that, but there were things I could only tell you face to face."

"You never have to apologize to me, Uncle. You have done more for me than I can ever repay," Xu said. "But as for Ava, is it really important to you that she and I develop a relationship?"

"It would bring me a sense of peace."

Xu held his glass out to Uncle. "Then I will do whatever is necessary to make it happen."

Uncle tapped the neck of his bottle against Xu's glass. "You have made me very happy."

"You haven't mentioned what she knows about me."

"I haven't told her anything about you, so that will be my next move. Ava is travelling on business right now. I expect her back in Hong Kong in a few days, and then I'll sit down with her and sing the song of Xu. When that's done, I would appreciate it if you could come to Hong Kong to meet her in person."

"I'd be glad to." Xu nodded somberly. "It will also give me another chance to spend time with you. And speaking of time together, we don't have to go to the factory tomorrow. If you prefer, you could come to the house, see Auntie Grace, and have a quiet dinner with us."

"That's very thoughtful, but truthfully I welcome the distraction the factory will offer," Uncle said, and then yawned. "Sorry, the day is beginning to catch up to me."

"I'll get going," Xu said, standing. "I'll call you in the morning when I'm close to the hotel. I would like to leave for the factory around ten."

"That works for me," said Uncle, rising to his feet.

They walked to the door. Xu reached for the handle, then turned and put his arms around Uncle. The two men hugged. Neither of them spoke.

8

WITHIN MINUTES OF XU LEAVING HIS SUITE, UNCLE climbed into bed. He was mentally and physically drained, and barely had the energy to take off his clothes. But it was with an overwhelming sense of relief that he pulled the duvet up to his chin.

He had hoped, but not taken for granted, that Xu would be amenable to his proposals. The fact that he had agreed to both was satisfying beyond words, and Uncle fell into a deep sleep with a sense of calm that had been absent from his life since his diagnosis. He slept soundly, and would certainly have slept longer if his mobile phone hadn't rung.

"*Wei*," he answered.

"It's Ava."

"Where are you?"

"I'm at the airport in Hong Kong."

"So soon?"

"Where are you?"

"I'm in Shanghai," he said.

"How are you feeling?"

"Well enough. I think we will be here for another day

at least. You did not have to rush back."

"I didn't come back for you," she said, and then quickly added: "That's not what I meant."

"There's no need to be concerned about my feelings," he said. "But you sounded distressed in your message, and now again you seem upset. Has something happened?"

"May and I have a problem in Kota Kinabalu, in Borneo. And now Amanda has been caught up in it."

"How?"

"She and one of our local partners in Borneo were attacked last night outside of a restaurant. They were beaten with baseball bats. We think it was premeditated," said Ava.

"What motivated the attack?"

"It's the money issue that Changxing alluded to when he called you, but it's too complicated to explain over the phone."

"Then you know who did it?"

"We think we know who was behind it, but we have no proof. I was hoping you could help get me some," she said. "I think the attackers were hired to do the job, and you don't just find men like that on the street, especially on short notice. So, if I wanted to hire someone in Kota Kinabalu for a job like that, who would I talk to?"

"I do not know."

"Can you find out?"

"Perhaps," Uncle said.

"All I need is a starting point — the name of someone who can point me in the right direction."

"I will speak to some people. I will get you a name."

"Thank you," said Ava.

"So you are going to Kota Kinabalu?"

"I am. May is already there. Amanda and our staff need our support."

Uncle had been lying down as he spoke to her, but now he sat up and swung his legs over the side of the bed. As self-sufficient as Ava could be, Kota Kinabalu did not seem to him to be a place where she and May should go it alone. "Ava, I am managing quite well here, and my hosts have been extremely supportive. Sonny has not been absolutely necessary —"

"I want Sonny to stay in Shanghai with you," she interrupted, immediately picking up on his suggestion. "It would be more of a worry for me knowing that you are by yourself."

"You might need help."

"If I do, I'll let you know. Right now, I just want to get things resolved, and then get back to Hong Kong in time for your return."

Uncle sighed but knew there was no point in arguing with her. "Sonny is only a few hours away if you require him."

"I know. Thank you."

"I will get the information you want within the next hour. Leave your phone on," he said.

"I don't have to board for another hour and a half, so I'll be here."

Uncle started to call Xu, and then stopped. His throat was dry, and he needed to go to the bathroom. There was nothing to lose, he decided, in taking a few minutes to gather himself. After a trip to the bathroom, he drank a glass of water, put on some clothes, and made a cup of coffee. He wasn't sure how the coffee would go down, so he took a careful sip and waited several seconds before taking another. When his stomach didn't feel bothered, he carried the cup to the desk and phoned Xu.

"Is this Uncle?" Auntie Grace answered.

"Yes, I hope this isn't too early to call," he said.

"It's almost eight. We've been up for ages," she said. "Wait a moment while I get Xu."

"Good morning, did you sleep well?" Xu asked when he came on the line.

"The best I have in some time."

"I'm glad to hear it. Have you changed your mind about visiting the factory?"

"No, I'm calling because I need your help — or actually, Ava does," Uncle said.

"I'd be pleased to help her however I can."

"Well, she's heading for Borneo this morning, to Kota Kinabalu, where they have made a business investment. Her partner, Amanda, and a local associate were attacked last night by some hired goons, and she wants to know who they work for. I was hoping you might have a name for me to give her."

"Not offhand, but let me phone the Mountain Master in Kuala Lumpur. Unless I'm mistaken, Kota is in one of the Malaysian states in Borneo, so he should know something."

"Thanks. Ava is at the airport in Hong Kong waiting for her flight."

"So, in other words, I should call KL right away," Xu said with a laugh.

"If you could, and I'm sorry for being so pushy."

"I'll do it as soon as we hang up," said Xu.

Uncle stayed at the desk. There was a time when he had known every Mountain Master in Asia. Those days were now gone, as death and retirement had created a new cadre of leaders. Fortunately, most of them had heard of Uncle, so his ability to get help wasn't too badly affected. But even when he was on top of his game, he had never heard the words

Borneo and *Mountain Master* in the same sentence. Was it possible the triads didn't have a presence in Kota Kinabalu?

He finished his coffee and called down for some congee from room service. As soon as he finished giving his order, his mobile rang.

"*Wei*," he answered.

"The man Ava needs to talk to is called Wan," Xu said quickly. "According to the Mountain Master in KL, Wan runs Kota Kinabalu."

"Is he triad?"

"It's not so easy to characterize. He has some kind of affiliation with 14K," Xu said, naming one of the largest triad gangs in the world. "But it was emphasized that he is not officially 14K and operates in Kota independently."

"What does 'affiliation' mean?"

"He buys drugs from them."

"So there is a relationship?"

"Of course. What is more difficult is determining how it is valued."

"By 14K?"

"No, by him," Xu said.

"He is that independent?"

"Yes, but mainly because no one cares about a market as small as Kota Kinabalu. He can do what he wants there as long as he pays for his drugs on time."

"Still…"

"My contact said that no one actually knows how to reach him. He calls them when he wants to place an order," Xu said. "Although my contact was told by his 14K source that he conducts much of his business in person from the Fa Pang Restaurant in Kota's downtown area. He's there most nights."

"That isn't much to go on."

"Wan runs a tight operation."

"How large is his gang?"

"There are about thirty members. Not all of them are active, but the gang casts a wide shadow and can pull in other men as needed."

"How wide?"

"In Borneo there are two Malaysian states, and each has their own operation. Wan is in Sabah state. The other is Sarawak and is run by a guy named Yeung. Wan and Yeung have a territorial agreement and a loose working relationship. They are both Hakka, though Wan has Sichuan roots and Yeung's family is from Fujian."

"I didn't realize the Chinese presence was so strong in Borneo," said Uncle.

"Me neither, but I was told the population is at least fifty percent Chinese and that Mandarin is commonly spoken."

"That should make it easier for Ava."

"Not necessarily. The KL Mountain Master stressed that Wan is very difficult to deal with."

"After everything you have told me, that is no surprise. I will let her know. Thank you, Xu — this will be of great help to Ava. I'll call her right away," Uncle said. "Then I'll meet you here at ten as planned."

He reached for a notepad, quickly jotted down the key points, and called Ava.

"Uncle, that was fast. Did you manage to find out what I asked?"

"Some of it," he said, and then relayed the information Xu had given him.

"In this day and age, how can someone be in business and

not be available by phone?" she asked when he had finished.

"I don't know. But Xu's contact believed you could find Wan at the restaurant."

"I guess that's my only option."

"Be careful."

"As always."

"And don't hesitate to contact me if you need more help," he said. "Remember, Sonny is only a short flight away."

"Uncle, I'll see you in Hong Kong in a couple of days. Please keep well," she said.

Uncle had an uneasy feeling when Ava ended their call. He had never believed in premonitions, but there was something about the situation in Borneo that ate at him. Missing money, hired goons with baseball bats attacking women on the street, a difficult gangster with some tenuous ties to the triads, and a place he knew nothing about. It was a mixture that made him so uncomfortable that he considered sending Sonny to join Ava even without her consent. Before that thought went any further, there was a loud knock at the door. He opened it to room service with his congee.

The congee was just as good as that of Morning Blessings — but at four times the price, Uncle thought that was the least it should be. Still, it was good, the portion was large, and eating carefully he managed to finish it all in half an hour. When he was done, his thoughts returned to Ava, Borneo, and Sonny. After a few minutes he shook his head in frustration. There was no way, he decided, that he could send Sonny without her permission. It would only irritate her. Besides, it was too late in their relationship for him to begin acting like a worried grandfather.

(9)

THEY DROVE IN TWO CARS TO NANTONG. UNCLE, XU,
and a driver went in the Mercedes, and they were followed by
Sonny, Suen, and two forty-niners in a BMW 8 Series sedan. It
was a 150-kilometre drive, and the plan was to arrive around
noon in time for lunch at the factory.

"Did you give Ava the information about Wan?" Xu asked
as they left the Peninsula in Shanghai.

"I did. And thank you again."

"Hopefully she can use it to resolve whatever problem
she has in Borneo."

"Speaking of her business," Uncle said, "I am confident
the Three Sisters will be successful in whatever they do, but
as substantial as their two hundred million start-up fund is,
it does rather limit their operations."

"What kind of operations are they planning?"

"So far, they've acquired a warehouse and logistics company in Shanghai. That's a sector that May knows very well,
and I know they want to expand their holdings in it. More
money would make that happen faster…"

"Are you suggesting that I invest money in the Three Sisters?"

"It is something to consider."

"As a partner?"

"No, I don't think the women would agree to that, but you could structure something on a deal-by-deal basis that precludes ownership but gives you a return on profit that reflects what would have been your percentage of partnership," said Uncle, and paused. "It is just an idea. I know you have an abundance of cash but few legitimate options to invest in. And I know the business arrangement I made with the Liu family in Shenzhen continues to provide the Fanling gang with returns that are not only consistent but legal. There are many advantages to being a silent partner with people you can trust."

"Have you discussed this with Ava and May Ling?"

"No, I wanted to gauge your interest first."

"It's true that we need to diversify in ways that will put our money to productive use without raising our profile or offending the authorities. Investing discreetly in legitimate businesses has considerable appeal."

"Then I will add that to my list of conversation topics when I speak to Ava in Hong Kong."

They were on the G40 Shanghai–Xi'an Expressway heading north to the Yangtze River. Nantong sat on its northern shore, and they would be crossing the seven-kilometre-long Chongming–Qidong Yangtze River Bridge to get there. Uncle looked out the window at rows of apartment blocks interspersed with factories and the occasional flash of greenery.

"I've never been to Nantong, but I remember how excited your father was when he opened his first clothing factory there."

"He copied what you were doing in Shenzhen, but it was a natural fit because Nantong was the leading textile manufacturer in China then. Textiles still form an important part of the city's economy, but after the government allowed it to accept foreign investment, new industries began popping up. Our factory was originally built to make small household appliances."

"What's the population now?"

"More than seven million."

"So finding good labour is not a problem?"

"That's the least of our worries. Our biggest problem is keeping our engineering and industrial design staff motivated. We have a mixture of young university grads, and talent we've poached from Apple and Samsung. They are a creative bunch and are always pushing to go in new directions."

"Like laptop computers?"

"Yes. I have little doubt we could make something almost as good as Apple, but I'm not convinced it will be profitable enough to justify the risk of infuriating the government. Apple has many friends in high places."

"I'm looking forward to the presentation."

Xu smiled. "I am as well. I've been kept in the dark until now."

The factory was on the outskirts of Nantong, in an industrial park that seemed to spread to hundreds of acres. Despite his familiarity with industrial parks in places like Shenzhen, Uncle couldn't remember seeing so many mammoth factories in one place. Some covered as much area as a city block, and there were buildings that were twenty storeys high. The signs on their walls identified a lot of textile manufacturers, but just as many were making appliances, bicycles, scooters, furniture, and unspecified electronics. When Xu's driver brought the car to a stop outside of a four-storey red-brick building, Uncle saw the sign — Ai Electronics — and smiled. Ai had been Xu's mother's name.

Before the driver could open the back door of the car, the front door of the building flew open and a large group of men and women gathered on the top three steps of the stone stairway.

"My management team," Xu said to Uncle as they got out, and just as the BMW arrived.

"Welcome, boss," a short, middle-aged man said, stepping forward.

"That's Mo," Xu said to Uncle. "He's the managing director and the comptroller. He was the assistant to my White Paper Fan until we decided it was more important for him to be here."

"Your timing is excellent. The food just arrived and is being set up in the executive boardroom."

"Thanks, Mo. I can't remember if you've met my guest, Uncle Chow Tung."

"I haven't, but I have heard of him," Mo said, bowing his head in Uncle's direction. "It is an honour to meet you."

"And I have heard how successful your business is, so I'm honoured to meet you as well."

Sonny and Suen joined them, and after Sonny was introduced to Mo, Xu touched Uncle lightly on the elbow and said, "We can go inside now."

The throng on the steps parted to let them pass, their heads slightly lowered.

"Would Uncle like to take a plant tour?" Mo asked Xu.

"Would you?" Xu looked to Uncle.

"I don't think so. I'm not the least bit technical and wouldn't know what I'm looking at."

"Then we'll go directly to the boardroom," Xu said to Mo.

They entered a large reception area that, in addition to two receptionists, had three armed guards positioned around it. Mo led them along a corridor to large wooden double doors with the words *Executive Boardroom* stencilled in gold. He opened them and stepped back.

Uncle hadn't known what to expect, but he now thought he could be walking into a buffet restaurant. There were ten seats around a long table, and each was set for lunch. On either side of the table, credenzas were covered with platters of food and a variety of drinks. There were five people already in the room, and Mo took the time to introduce all of them. One was his deputy managing director, and the others represented the marketing, design, production, and finance departments.

"Why don't we eat, and then we can begin the presentation," said Mo.

There were at least ten separate dishes to choose from, but Uncle decided to be cautious and stuck to rice with crab. Xu picked at a few more dishes, while Sonny and Suen filled their plates several times. They all drank beer, except for Uncle who drank water.

When lunch ended and the table had been cleared, Mo turned to Xu. "Where do you want us to start? I believe our team can speak to any question you might have."

"The most basic one is why should we start manufacturing laptops?" Xu asked.

"I will ask the head of marketing to speak to that," said Mo.

Uncle knew only the basics about computer production, and had no concept of the size or value of the market. The numbers related by the marketing head were staggering. Apple had been experiencing double-digit growth for several years, and the previous year its sales had topped two hundred billion dollars. The MacBook Pro — which the Ai design team had targeted to duplicate — was Apple's priority product in the sector, and appeared to be positioned for continuing growth.

The director of technical design spoke next. His engineers had identified every part of the MacBook Pro and estimated it could be made for about seven hundred dollars. The component parts were all available for Ai to purchase.

"But wait a minute," Xu said. "Marketing just told us that Apple is selling that device in the eleven-hundred- to twelve-hundred-dollar range. How can we undercut them and make a profit with those costs?"

The director smiled, and said, "Perhaps Mr. Mo should explain."

Now it was Mo's turn to smile. "The most expensive component in the MacBook is the processor, at around three hundred dollars. Our technical engineering and design teams have been able to create a processor in-house that will work just as well — or almost as well — and costs only one hundred dollars. That gives us the financial breathing room we need."

"Okay, and if we decide to go ahead with this project, can we do it without interfering with phone production?" Xu asked.

"We could figure out something for the short term with limited output, but if we want to do volume, we will have to build an addition to our existing facility. We have prepared some preliminary plans with timelines," Mo said.

As Mo began to outline those plans, Uncle's attention began to wane. There was a time when he couldn't get enough information, but that had been ten years ago when he was still running a gang and the several large businesses they owned. Now, despite caring for Xu, he was finding it difficult to get excited about a product that he had no real interest in. His mind began to wander, and when he glanced at Sonny and Suen he thought they had tuned out Mo as well.

They left Ai Electronics at just past three o'clock, and Uncle could barely remember anything that had been said during the last hour.

"I'm sorry the meeting went so long," Xu said as he and Uncle got into the car. "With all our key people in one room, it was the perfect time to ask all the questions I had."

"And I apologize if I appeared inattentive. I seem to have lost my appetite for detail, and truthfully I started to feel a little tired."

"Sit back and relax," said Xu. "You can nap on the drive back to Shanghai."

Uncle laid his head against the seat. "What time are you meeting Fu tonight?"

"Eight o'clock. We were planning to go to a steakhouse. Would you like to join us?"

"Fu won't mind?"

"I wouldn't care if he did, but I don't think that will be the case," said Xu. "He respects you, and he knows we're close."

"Can I put off making a decision until later?"

"Sure."

Uncle closed his eyes. In retrospect, attending the meeting

had been unnecessary, and perhaps a mistake, as it had taxed his energy considerably. He had come to Shanghai to accomplish a set of objectives, and the talks last night and this morning in the car with Xu had done that. What else was there left to do? He had been running on adrenalin that — like everything else associated with his health — wasn't as plentiful as it used to be. He just hoped he had enough in reserve to get back to Hong Kong and finish building the bridge between Ava and Xu.

10

IT WAS PAST SIX WHEN THEY FINALLY REACHED THE
Peninsula Hotel. Uncle had slept during the ride, but it hadn't
bolstered his energy. In fact, he felt as tired as he'd been when
he was taking chemotherapy.

"Xu," he said as the car came to a stop. "I don't think I can
go to the dinner with Fu. I need rest more than food. Please
pass along my apologies to him."

"That isn't necessary, but I'm concerned about you. Is
there anything I can do?"

"No, all I need is a good night's rest."

"Will you be leaving tomorrow?"

"I expect that I will."

"If you're feeling up to it, do you think you could join
Auntie Grace and me for breakfast tomorrow morning?
I know she would love to see you."

"I would like to see her too. Let's see how I am then. I'll
call you first thing to let you know."

Xu got out of the car and motioned to Sonny to join them.
"Uncle isn't feeling terrific. We may have taken on more than

we should the last few days. Stay in touch with me. I want to know how he's doing."

"I don't need a babysitter," said Uncle.

"I didn't mean to offend you," Xu said quickly. "But you don't realize sometimes how much we all care about you."

"Things are what they are, and no amount of care can change that," Uncle said, and regretted it immediately when he saw how Xu and Sonny reacted. He laid a hand on Xu's arm. "I'm sorry. I'm just beyond tired. My bones ache, my legs feel like they are filled with lead, and my head is mush."

Xu gripped his hand. "Get a good night's rest. If I see you in the morning, I'll be thrilled. If I don't, then hopefully I'll see you in Hong Kong and have a chance to meet Ava."

"That sounds like an excellent plan," said Uncle.

He waited until Xu got into his car before entering the hotel, with Sonny hovering at his side.

"I hate to see you like this, boss," said Sonny.

"No more than I hate feeling like this," Uncle said. "But listen, I don't want you hanging around the hotel tonight worrying about me. Go out with Suen or some other of Xu's men. Just keep your phone on so I can get hold of you if I need you."

Five minutes later Uncle entered his suite, and paused near the door as a feeling of being in a place where he didn't belong came over him. *This day just gets stranger and stranger*, he thought. Still, as illogical as it seemed, he checked the bedroom to make sure his bag was there, and when he saw it was, he went to the living room and sat on the couch. He took his phone out and turned it on for the first time since that morning, and checked for messages. There were none, so he could only assume Ava had landed safely in Borneo.

Without much enthusiasm, he turned on the television and found a variety show on China Central Television. He watched a juggling act, and then to his surprise a rather tall comedian took the stage. His name was Dashan, which meant "Big Mountain." But it wasn't his height or name that caught Uncle off guard; it was the fact he was a westerner, a Canadian, who spoke such impeccable Mandarin that, when Uncle closed his eyes, he could have sworn he was listening to a well-educated Chinese. Dashan's nationality brought thoughts about Ava back into Uncle's head, and almost as a reflex, he called her.

Her phone rang six times before going to voicemail, which he found unusual. Typically, if Ava didn't want to be contacted, she turned off her phone. If it was on, she nearly always answered. Uncle wondered if he was just being overly protective, overly sensitive, or maybe just paranoid. In any event, it wasn't something he was prepared to ignore. He called May Ling.

"*Wei*," she answered in a voice that sounded strained.

"This is Uncle. I've been trying to contact Ava without success. Is everything okay over there?"

"I don't know," she said. "I've been waiting to hear from her."

"I called her cell phone. It was on, but she didn't answer, which isn't like her. Do you know where she is?"

"Since she arrived, she has spent her time trying to get a meeting with Wan. She finally managed to connect with him this afternoon. She told me that they worked out some kind of deal."

"What deal?"

"We want to know who hired the men who attacked Amanda Yee and Chi-Tze, our partner in the furniture business," May said. "Wan told Ava that he knew who did it, and that he would give us the names for a price. She left here an hour ago with one hundred thousand ringgit — about twenty-five thousand U.S. dollars."

"And you haven't heard from her since?" Uncle asked, feeling his stomach begin to constrict.

"No."

"Where was she meeting Wan? Was it far from the hotel?"

"She went to a restaurant on the waterfront, no more than five minutes from the hotel."

"Fa Pang?"

"Yes, that's the one."

So many questions flooded his mind that Uncle hardly knew where to begin. After a pause, he asked, "Why did Ava go to the meeting alone?"

"I offered to go with her, but Wan told her to come alone," May said quickly, and Uncle realized she might have found his question accusatory.

"May, I wasn't implying that you did anything wrong. I was simply trying to understand."

"For the last fifteen minutes I have been wondering what's keeping her, and I've actually been thinking about going to the restaurant myself to check."

"Do you have someone who can go with you? An employee, or maybe someone from the hotel?"

"I could talk to hotel security to see if they would help."

"That is a very good idea," said Uncle.

"Let me do that right now, and then I'll call you back."

"If you have to pay security to help, don't hesitate to do it."

"Uncle, I do understand how the world works," May said, sounding slightly offended.

"Of course you do, and I apologize for stating the obvious. I'm just worried about Ava. I know it may be irrational, but irrationality seems to accompany my current medical condition."

"Uncle, I'm worried as well, and I don't think either of us are the least bit irrational."

"Thank you for that, May. It makes me feel less unhinged. Now, please go call security. I'll be waiting," he said.

Uncle put down the phone and grabbed a bottle of beer from the minibar. His mouth was dry, so he took a sip and swirled the liquid around his mouth before swallowing it. It didn't help, and he knew his nerves wouldn't settle until he knew Ava was all right. He wondered if Sonny had left the hotel and if he should put him on standby. But standby for what? All he knew for certain was that Ava was in Borneo and had a meeting with Wan. Why should he believe the meeting had gone badly when it could just as easily have gone well? His phone rang and he saw May Ling's number.

"What did security say?" he asked before she could speak.

"I didn't talk to them. There was no need. Ava's not at the restaurant," she said, her voice breaking.

"What has happened?" he asked.

"I got a call from Ava's phone, except it wasn't her on the line; it was a man named Kang," said May. "I asked him if he was at the restaurant with Ava. He laughed and said no. Then I asked him if he worked with Wan. He said yes and that he had a business proposition to pass along."

Uncle's head began to spin as he realized where this was going. "How much do they want for her?" he asked.

"How did you know?"

"How much?"

"Two million ringgit."

"What did you tell Kang?"

"That I would have to get back to him. I said I had part-ners I had to consult."

"How did he react?"

"Not well, but he gave me an hour."

"This is my fault," Uncle blurted. "I should never have given her Wan's name before checking him out thoroughly. Once Ava agreed to pay him for the information, he probably figured there was more to be had."

"You couldn't have known, Uncle," May said.

"The point is I shouldn't have sent her into that kind of situation without proper backup," he said. "There was a day when I would have done that automatically."

May hesitated, and in her silence Uncle sensed she agreed with him. But all she said was, "What do we do now?"

"First, you need to demand proof that Ava is alive and unharmed. A phone call from her would suffice," he said. "Next, you need to buy as much time as you can. They'll want the money in cash, so tell them you can't get that amount until the banks open in the morning."

"Uncle, are you suggesting we pay them?"

"Of course we pay them, but there has to be a physical exchange. We hand them the money; they give us Ava."

"What if they won't agree?"

"If you have to concede something, give way on the exchange. Time is what we need most right now."

11

UNCLE'S HAND WAS SHAKING WHEN HE PUT DOWN THE phone after speaking with May Ling. Why had he given Wan's name to Ava without looking into him first? Why hadn't he insisted that Sonny go to Borneo? He took several deep breaths and then called Sonny's cell.

"Yes, boss," he answered.

"Where are you?"

"I'm with Suen. We just left the hotel."

"Come back, and bring Suen with you. Come to my room."

"Yes, boss."

Uncle's next call was to Xu.

"Uncle, have you changed your mind about joining us for dinner?" Xu asked.

"No, I have a problem that I need your help with. Sonny and Suen are together, and I've asked them to come to my room. I would appreciate it very much if you could come as well."

"This sounds serious," Xu said.

"It is."

"I'll be there in fifteen minutes," said Xu.

"Thank you."

Uncle wondered how May Ling was doing. He knew that she was a good negotiator, but that was in business, where personal emotions weren't necessarily involved. He began to pace back and forth across the room. He had some experience with hostage situations; they rarely ended well. How could he ensure this one did? As he was considering his options, there was a knock at the door. He opened it to find Sonny and Suen looking down at him with faces full of concern.

"Come in and take a seat. Xu will be joining us shortly," Uncle said. He followed them into the suite, and after they sat he headed for the bathroom. "I'll be back in a few minutes."

He splashed cold water on his face, and then sat on the toilet as he continued to gather his thoughts. There was only one acceptable outcome, and he knew that half measures wouldn't achieve it. But how far could he go? How much could he ask of Xu?

A knock on the bathroom door brought him back to the present, and Sonny said, "Boss, Xu is here."

"My apologies for dragging you away from your dinner with Fu," Uncle said when he returned to the living room.

"Never mind the dinner; tell me what has happened," Xu said.

"Ava has been kidnapped by Wan's gang in Kota Kinabalu. They are demanding the equivalent of half a million U.S. dollars as a ransom," Uncle said as calmly as he could. "Ava's friend May Ling — who is in Kota with her — is negotiating with them as we speak."

"Negotiating what exactly?" Xu asked, exhibiting calm.

"I asked her to stall for time, and to insist that Ava and the money be exchanged simultaneously."

"That isn't how these things usually work," Suen said, glancing nervously at Xu.

"I am aware that sometimes the money is paid before the hostage is released, but just as often the money is paid and then the hostage is killed," said Uncle.

"Even if the hostage and ransom-payers swear not to go to the cops, some of the gangs who do this shit won't take the chance. Their best protection is to make sure there are no witnesses," said Suen.

"I understand their reasoning," Uncle said. "I also understand that they can't be trusted to hold up their end of any agreement. So paying them a ransom and then hoping that they will release Ava is not something I am prepared to do."

"Do those fuckers know who they're dealing with?" Sonny asked.

"I have no idea what Ava told them, but even if she told them about me, what weight would that carry? They have probably never heard of me, and if they have, they'll know I've been out of the game for years."

"I can't imagine they haven't heard of Xu," Suen said. "If Wan knew that you had his support, that might make a difference."

"It might, but how do we deliver that message to a man who doesn't use a phone?" Uncle asked.

"Maybe he needs to be told in person," Xu said, and then looked at Suen. "We were told that Wan has about thirty men in his gang. How many of our men would you need to bring them to heel?"

"I could probably get by with ten of our best."

"Then take fifteen. How soon can you have them organized and ready to go?"

"I would need three or four hours."

Xu nodded and took out his phone. He hit a number, waited for a few seconds, and said, "Feng, I'm sorry to bother you at home, but I need you to do something for me. I'm sending Suen and fifteen of our men to Kota Kinabalu in Borneo to sort out a problem, and I need to get them there as quickly as possible. How long will it take you to charter a plane?"

Uncle could hear Feng say something but couldn't make out the words.

"Yes, I would like them to go tonight, and I don't care about the expense," Xu continued. "Call me back when it's done."

Uncle stared at him. "Xu, this is more than I had any right to expect. I don't know how to thank you."

"It is too soon for thanks. Let's wait until we get Ava out of Wan's clutches," said Xu, turning to Suen. "Start rounding up your men and weapons."

"Yes, sir," said Suen.

"I want to go with them," Sonny said to Uncle.

"Is that a problem?" Uncle asked Xu.

"Of course not. I'm sure Suen will be pleased to have him along."

"I don't have a gun with me," Sonny said.

"I'll get you one," said Suen.

"Taking weapons onto a plane won't be a problem?" Uncle asked Xu.

"We fly most of our phones to market on private planes, and we have developed a strong working relationship with the customs officials at the airport. There won't be a problem there, and they will make sure we don't have a problem when we land."

Uncle shook his head. "That's an amazing business model you've created."

"Making partners of government officials — even indirectly — is a strategy I learned from my father, and he told me he learned it from you."

"I —" Uncle began, then stopped when his phone rang. "May, did you speak to Kang? Did you convince them to wait?"

"Yes, they'll wait until tomorrow morning. The banks open at ten. They want their money by eleven," she said, her voice breaking.

"Did you discuss the exchange with them?"

"Yes, and Kang didn't say no, but he sort of brushed it off by saying they wouldn't commit to anything until they knew for certain that we had the cash."

"I expected something like that," Uncle said. "What about Ava? Did they let you speak to her?"

"Oh, Uncle," she sobbed suddenly.

"What!"

"All they let her say was, 'This is Ava and I'm okay.' Kang sent me a photo of her," she said, her crying intensifying.

"Have they hurt her?" he asked, rising to his feet.

"She was tied to a chair in what looked like a warehouse."

"But have they hurt her?"

"Her eyes were blindfolded, and there was blood on her face, but she looked determined not to give in," May said, then hesitated.

"What aren't you telling me?"

May sobbed again and blurted, "Her blouse is open, and a breast is exposed. I can't help thinking the worst."

Uncle felt his heart skip a beat and his stomach contract. He reached down and put his hand on the back of the chair to steady himself. "May, we are sending a crew to Borneo tonight. Sonny is going with them. These aren't men to mess with. They will get Ava, and they will make those bastards pay for any harm they have done to her."

"We can't lose her."

"We won't."

"What should I do now?"

"Wait in the hotel. We'll contact you when this is over and Ava is free."

"I don't know how I'm going to sleep. I can't get that photo out of my mind."

"Just tell yourself that things are going to work out," he said.

"I'll try."

Uncle ended the call, and then saw that Xu, Sonny, and Suen were staring at him intently. "Ava seems to be okay," he said slowly.

"But you mentioned 'harm.' Have they hurt her?" asked Xu.

The image of Ava tied to a chair leapt into Uncle's mind, and he felt his head get even lighter. "Do whatever it takes to get her back. I don't care if you have to kill them all to do it."

"You know there's nothing we won't do," Sonny said. "We'll get her back, boss."

Uncle nodded, lifted his hand from the back of the chair, and took two faltering steps in the direction of the bathroom before his legs gave way. He blacked out before he hit the floor.

12

UNCLE WAS CONFUSED. HE THOUGHT HE MIGHT BE IN a dream. He could hear voices, some of them familiar, but when he tried to see who was speaking, he couldn't open his eyes. And when he tried to call out, he couldn't make a sound. He was pretty sure he was lying on his back, but couldn't understand why he felt like he was being lifted into the air.

When he was finally able to open his eyes, he quickly closed them again to shut out the glare of an overhead light. He waited for a few seconds and tried again, covering his eyes with the back of a wrist from which an IV tube protruded. "Where am I?" he asked hoarsely. There was no answer.

He lay like that for several minutes until he heard a door open. He lifted his wrist from his eyes and saw a nurse walking towards him. "Where am I?" he asked.

"The Queen Elizabeth Hospital in Kowloon," she said.

"How did I get here?"

"Doctor Parker should be the one to explain that to you," she said. "He asked me to call him if... rather, *when* you woke."

"Then please tell him I'm awake," Uncle said, surprised

at the effort it took.

He closed his eyes again and started to drift away, his mind filled with random and unconnected thoughts.

"Mr. Chow...Uncle," a voice said.

His eyelids were heavy, and he had to force them open. Doctor Parker stood by the side of the bed.

"I recognize you, and I know where I am, but I don't remember how I got here," Uncle said.

"You were flown here from Shanghai very early this morning in a private plane. You were accompanied by a friend and attended to by a very capable nurse."

"Which friend?"

"His name is Xu. He is still in Hong Kong. I'm to call him once we know your situation."

"What is that situation?"

Parker placed a hand on the bed. "I'm afraid it isn't very good. I thought we were going to lose you. Mr. Xu explained that you might have overdone things physically in Shanghai, and on top of that, you suffered some kind of emotional blow. Those things, combined with your cancer, brought on a stroke that has damaged your heart."

"Ava — my granddaughter..." Uncle said, as memories began to surface.

"Yes, Mr. Xu said it involved her."

"What's the time?" Uncle asked.

"Just after eight a.m."

A memory intruded of Sonny and Suen going to Borneo, and then Uncle realized he couldn't be sure they had gone. Had they found a plane? If they had, when had they left, how long was the flight, had they landed, and most important, what were they doing now? Had they found Ava?

"Where is Xu?" he asked.

"He told me he was going to check into the Peninsula Hotel."

"I need to talk to him," he said to Parker.

"I'd prefer that you didn't. I'm worried what the additional stress might do," Parker said. "Besides, Mr. Xu told me that you were waiting for news on the subject that triggered your stroke, and he promised to call me the moment he heard anything. I assure you that I haven't missed any calls from him, and that the moment I hear from him I'll pass along his news."

"They have to be there by now," Uncle muttered.

"What?"

"Nothing, but if you don't hear from Xu in the next hour, could you please call him for me?"

"Yes, I can do that," Parker said. "Now you need to rest."

Uncle took a deep breath, and when he exhaled, he could feel his body's energy draining away. His eyes started to close, and he fought to keep them open. He needed to stay awake, he thought, suddenly fearful that his next sleep could be his last.

He lay still, not moving a muscle, his body disconnected from his brain, and his brain slowly circulated memories of Gui-San and Ava. Despite his best efforts, he did eventually fall asleep, but woke when the nurse came to change his IV bag.

"What's in there?" he asked.

"You need hydration, plus there are some painkillers and a mild sedative."

"What's the time?"

"It isn't quite nine."

When had time ever passed so slowly, he wondered. "Could you ask Doctor Parker to come see me?" he asked.

The nurse hesitated, then turned and said, "There's no need for that. Here he is now."

Parker smiled as he approached the bed. "I just called Mr. Xu. He said to tell you that the men have landed; the project is well underway; and that the initial results are encouraging."

"Ava?"

"He didn't mention her specifically."

"Thank you anyway."

"Now rest. All this worry is not doing you any good."

Xu wouldn't lie about that, Uncle thought, not even if Xu was doing it to protect him from bad news. So things had to be going well. And why wouldn't they? The local gangsters would be no match for Suen's men, and an unleashed, angry Sonny was a fearsome sight. They would find her, he told himself, and they would rescue her. Then the image that May had implanted in his head of Ava tied to a chair with her shirt undone flooded over him. *Oh God, let that be all they did to her*, he thought, as tears began trickling down his cheeks.

Suddenly, a pain erupted in his chest that caused him to gasp. It took minutes for the pain to subside, and even then it didn't disappear completely. He considered calling for the nurse, but to what end? It didn't matter now. All he needed was to last a few more hours, he thought as he fell asleep again.

When he awoke, Parker stood over him.

"Did you talk to Xu again?" he asked.

"No, I did one better. I spoke to your granddaughter,"

Parker said. "Ava called the hospital and was put through to me."

"What did she say?"

"A great many things — she's safe and she intends to return to Hong Kong as quickly as possible. She wants you to be here when she arrives," Parker said. "And of course, she wanted me to tell you she loves you."

Uncle sighed so deeply that he found it difficult to find a return breath.

"I know that's the news you wanted to hear, and I hope it eases some of the stress you've been experiencing."

Uncle nodded. "Thank you," he whispered.

He felt an overpowering sense of relief wash over him, followed by a pain in his chest. Uncle closed his eyes.

(EPILOGUE)

UNCLE COULDN'T REMEMBER LEAVING THE HOSPITAL, but when he opened his eyes again, he was standing in front of Dong's Restaurant in Fanling.

The door was closed, and he couldn't see past it, but he could hear voices. He turned the handle and stepped inside, to be met immediately by Dong.

"We were wondering when you would get here. Let me take you to your table," Dong said.

The restaurant was busy, and there was a surprisingly large number of familiar faces, including some people Uncle hadn't seen in years.

"Come and sit with us," one of his former Mountain Masters said.

Uncle stared at him, confused because he thought the man was dead. After a slight pause, he started to follow Dong again towards the rear of the restaurant.

"Tian is here, and your old friend Xu," Dong said. "They are anxious to see you."

"Did Xu come all the way from Shanghai?" Uncle asked.

"I'm not sure. He didn't say."

"Chow," a voice shouted.

Uncle froze.

"Chow, I am over here."

Uncle looked in the direction of the voice, and saw Gui-San waving at him from the corner. He walked towards her with his heart racing.

"How did you know to meet me here?" he asked.

She smiled.

ACKNOWLEDGEMENTS

The Uncle books were initially conceived as a trilogy, but as I completed the third book in the series — *Fortune* — it became clear to me that I couldn't leave Uncle's story unfinished. Fortunately, my publisher agreed that a fourth book was appropriate. But knowing I wanted to write a fourth Uncle novel and actually writing it were two different things.

My first thought was to write *Finale* in three separate sections, spanning roughly ten years and mirroring the Ava Lee books, *The Dragon Head of Hong Kong*, *The Scottish Banker of Surabaya*, and *The Two Sisters of Borneo*. It was a hefty manuscript, and ultimately felt like too slow a read. My editor Doug Richmond and I talked it over, and I made the decision to discard over one hundred pages — nearly all related to *The Dragon Head* — and to build some of the backstory into the other two sections. That gave us the book you've just read.

The other challenge was deciding how precisely I should mirror *The Scottish Banker* and *The Two Sisters*. The events in those books were seen through Ava's eyes, while in *Finale* they are seen through Uncle's. I decided to maintain the plots and all their details but made some adjustments to dialogue and reinterpreted the characters' emotional reactions. My rationale was that no two people experience or remember things the same, and that Uncle's recollection of a conversation with Ava might well be different than hers.

So that is the background to this book.

A huge thanks, as always, to Doug for his editorial and emotional support, and to House of Anansi for continuing to believe in my work.

Finale went to fewer first readers than usual, only because I had so many doubts about the manuscript and didn't feel quite ready to share it. But my first reader of first readers, my wife Lorraine, did provide her usual insightful input. And my friend Robin Spano accurately pinpointed many weaknesses in the first draft. A big thanks and a hug to each of them.

IAN HAMILTON is the acclaimed author of fourteen books in the Ava Lee series, four in the Lost Decades of Uncle Chow Tung series, and the standalone novel *Bonnie Jack*. His books have been shortlisted for numerous prizes, including the Arthur Ellis Award, the Barry Award, and the Lambda Literary Prize, and are national bestsellers. BBC Culture named Hamilton one of the ten mystery/crime writers from the last thirty years who should be on your bookshelf. The Ava Lee series is being adapted for television.

ALSO AVAILABLE
from House of Anansi Press

The Lost Decades of Uncle Chow Tung

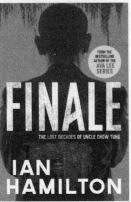

NOW AVAILABLE
from House of Anansi Press
The Ava Lee series

Prequel and Book 1

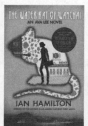

Book 2

Book 3

Book 4

Book 5

Book 6

Book 7

Book 8

Book 9

Book 10

Book 11

Book 12

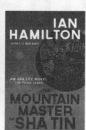

Book 13

Book 14

www.houseofanansi.com • www.facebook.com/avaleenovels
www.ianhamiltonbooks.com • www.twitter.com/avaleebooks

ALSO AVAILABLE
from House of Anansi Press

"Hamilton, author of the Ava Lee mystery series, turns in a stellar performance in this stand-alone…Hamilton pulls us into the story with carefully crafted characters, and keeps us involved by increasing the complexity of the tale: introducing a mystery here, uncorking a shocking revelation there. The book is a departure from the author's more traditional mystery fiction, but his fans will find much here that is familiar: realistic dialogue, characters they can care about, and a gripping story." —*Booklist*

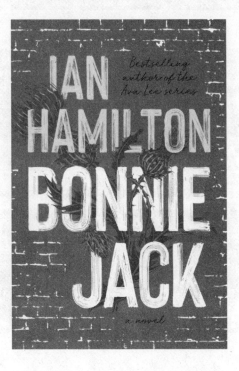

www.houseofanansi.com
www.ianhamiltonbooks.com